The enemy, he  *enemy.*

But still, his heart tripped. Tripped again. A deep breath in, then out. It made little difference. He could not hold another thought in his head. His only purpose now, was to kiss her.

And what harm would a kiss cause?

He could think of nothing.

"Fine. I confess," she whispered. "I'd rather have a kiss for my reward. Okay? Are you happy now?"

Was he happy? He was in hell. And her speaking aloud of the kiss he was determined to take? It should sober him. He should turn and put space between them. He should walk about in the snow outside, perhaps with his feet bare, to remember his purpose. And still, he advanced.

She hid her shaking hands behind her back and waited. When the toes of his stockinged feet mingled with hers, he leaned down, breathing her in. He measured the moment, tucking each rise of her chest into his memory, to relive later.

How sad, that it would all be relegated to memory.

With his mouth an inch from hers, he murmured, "There was no date on the letter lass. I win. I claim my prize."

Their lips brushed past, then returned, hers pressing forward as much as his. But he wanted to ensure she would remember it, this one and only kiss between them. He teased, sipped the taste of her, his lips a whisper against her own, then he pressed in again, renewing the heat they'd begun with, stealing her breath away.

Then he stepped back and did the only thing that would ensure it would never happen again...

CHRISTMAS KISS

By L. L. Muir

PUBLISHED BY

IVY&STONE

www.llmuir.weebly.com

CHRISTMAS KISS © 2012 Lesli Muir Lytle
All rights reserved

This book is a work of fiction. The names, characters, places, and incidents are products of the writer's imagination or have been used fictitiously and are not to be construed as real. Any resemblance to persons, living or dead, actual events, locales or organizations is entirely coincidental.

Cover Art © 2012 Kelli Ann Morgan
www.inspirecreativeservices.com

Interior Book Design by
Bob Houston eBook Formatting
http://about.me/BobHouston

ISBN: 9781480098060

Dedication

To Marli,

my sister and my friend,

who laughs in all the right spots.

PROLOGUE

———✦———

Highlands of Scotland, 1806

Heathcliff McKinnon, reclusive Laird of the McKinnons, stood alone in the arched window of the East tower, the shutters flung wide with no fear of the coming storm. His calloused hands gripped the ledge in desperation as if he were hanging from it instead of standing safely inside the stones of his own home. He'd made this tower his private sanctuary long ago. Tonight, it wasn't enough.

He threw back his head and faced the plump white moon. An ominous size that night, it held back a wall of gathering clouds as if waiting for some signal to allow the army of snow to attack the peaceful village below. As if waiting for a signal from *him*.

"Help me! God. Odin. Anyone." Heathcliff whispered. "I'd give all I have."

The moonlight pulsed and the wind stirred. Brighter clouds pushed 'round the orb and spilled into the sky like milk poured into water. The crumbling battlements below were lit for a moment, then were gone, for in no time at all, the thickening clouds had blocked the light.

The storm was upon him. Large wet snowflakes flew into his shirt and melted it to his chest, but still he held onto the ledge as if the brawn of his arms might save him from despair. When the cold began slipping past his body and into his home, he finally accepted that his pleas would go unanswered...

For surely, the storm could be no help at all.

CHAPTER ONE

Scotland, December, Present Day

Surprised to still be alive, Bree Colby sat in her rental car, gripping the steering wheel and staring at the tilted landscape for one very long minute before she realized the vehicle was filling with water.

This can't be happening.
This can't be happening.
This can't be happening.

But it was.

Water leaked around the edges of the passenger door. And, thanks to her still-functioning headlights, she realized the dark patches in the snow in front of her were signs of a half-frozen stream. And she'd be half-frozen in two minutes if she didn't start moving!

The seatbelt had probably saved her, but it had become her biggest threat. She pushed herself hard against the back of the seat and lifted the release, but she ended up tumbling anyway, sideways, head-first toward the water. Her hands hit the submerged glass of the passenger window, and it took all her strength to catch herself, but only the ends of her hair got wet. Her head might be filling with blood, but at least she wasn't drowning in four inches of water.

She had two new problems, though. Her hands were starting to tingle from the icy water and she could feel the glass screaming; it was going to shatter!

She hooked her knees on the steering wheel and pulled as much of her weight as possible off her hands. Then she pulled her way back up the dashboard until she could grasp the steering wheel again. Unfortunately, it spun around and her knees slipped. She hung on for dear life, but she couldn't stop her bottom half from falling. When her feet landed in the water, she was grateful she was at least right side up.

The glass was not so grateful.

She didn't know where the strength came from, but as her footing fell away, she pulled and jumped. Her feet landed on the seat and she tried to climb it. The steering wheel was no help at all. The tires were obviously in the air and there was nothing to keep the damn wheel from spinning every time she gained a step. But even if she could climb, there was a very heavy car door above her and that window was still intact.

She was going to die. And at her funeral, her mother would place a big ribbon across her casket that would read, "I told you so."

How sad. She had crashed in a foreign country, miles from any town, late at night, and she dreaded her mother's reaction more than freezing to death. The woman had forbidden her to go to Scotland alone, especially at Christmas time when she should be with her family. But Bree had to take control of her life sometime. It might as well be during the holiday break when it wouldn't interrupt with her teaching job. Besides, she had to make sure her mother understood that just because Bree had stopped letting David manipulate her didn't mean she would hand control back to her mother. Bree was in control of her life from now on...

Even if she drove herself into a ditch.

It was too late, of course, but she realized she should have refused to take a rental car that didn't have snow tires, especially when it was snowing when she was handed the key. But the old clunker had been the only option and she'd been so mortified she couldn't wait to get out of that little town.

But old clunkers wouldn't have electric windows!

She looked over her shoulder, into the shadows, and found the window crank. If it worked, she might even consider forgiving the old man that rented her the car—in spite of the fact she'd insisted.

Her eye caught on her large plaid purse. At least some of the squares were visible in the near darkness. She grabbed it and pulled the handle over her shoulder.

The glove box was open, so she stuck a foot inside it, then she made sure her other foot was stuck firmly between the seats before she reached for the crank. No way was she going back into the water. She was afraid one more icy splash might be one too many. Already, she was so cold she felt the fight draining out of her.

She pulled with everything she had, but the window didn't budge. Terror flooded her lungs. She really was going to die!

Then she realized she might be turning it the *wrong way!*

She said a prayer while she pushed, and the crank turned easily. The window came down, inch by inch, and by the time she was done, her hands had warmed up a little too. Thanks to her coat and jeans, only her feet and hands were in danger of freezing at the moment.

She stretched up and found the car handle on the outside of the door, then wrapped her fingers around it and clamped down tight. If her hand froze, it would at least be frozen in a helpful place. Using the seats and the dashboards like ladders, she finally climbed out of the hole, but she still wasn't going to let go of the handle.

The car was slippery from the constant snowfall and she was surrounded by water.

While she took a minute to catch her breath, she noticed the wind blowing against her face wasn't nearly as frigid as she'd expected. It was almost warm. A large puffy snowflake stuck to her hand and melted immediately. Maybe she wasn't going to die after all.

The trunk was open and above water, but she wasn't going to tempt fate. With her luck, she'd jump down into it and the lid would mysteriously close.

The tingling in her feet reminded her that the cute red rain boots were in the suitcase, in that trunk, and if she could get to them, it might save her toes. She also had a cell phone in her purse that might just work in the Highlands of Scotland. But even if she could figure out Britain's version of 911, she could easily freeze before anyone could get to her.

No. She was on her own, for a while at least. And she needed those boots.

She stretched out on the cold wet metal and scooted toward the trunk to take a peek inside. She didn't dare move fast. She was shaky and a good shiver might throw her off balance. She had to stay centered.

The last normal thing she remembered was cautiously making her way through the snow storm and reminding herself that the white stuff was just going to make the holiday in Scotland that much more picturesque. But then a burst of wind, or a mean-spirited fairy, had shoved at the front fender and sent her spinning.

If only she'd swallowed her pride and waited until morning... But the little man had sounded just like her mother. If only he hadn't used the word *foolish*.

As it turned out, she'd been scammed by the Heart of Scotland Tour Company and discovered it five minutes before the man at the rental office used her mother's eff word. He thought she was silly to want to leave his humble town so late on a winter's day, but she'd felt desperate to get to the next town where no one would know what a sucker she'd been. No way did she want to sit around a pub wondering who the bartender might have told or waiting for someone to cajole her into telling her pitiful tale.

She'd taken the train from Heathrow Airport and arrived in the little town of Burnshire right on schedule. The tour was supposed to start at the Will o' the Wisp Pub at four o'clock that afternoon. They were to check into a Bed and Breakfast, next door, before dinner. Unfortunately, the big man at the Pub had never heard of the tour company and there was no Bed and Breakfast next door.

The bartender assured her she was welcomed to let a room from his sister down the road. But in her shock, the only words that fell off her tongue were, "Where can I rent a car?"

It had been a natural reaction, she realized hours later. She was a car girl. Since she'd turned 16 and gotten her first car, her car was her private space, her safe space. There were locks on the doors; she was able to think clearly in a space where she could lock out the rest of the world. And clear thinking was what she'd needed. Unfortunately, the Scottish car hadn't turned out to be her safe place in the end.

Foolish? Yeah, probably. But you can't fight someone's knee-jerk reaction. Other people had "fight or flight" instincts. Hers were more like "fight or flee in a car."

She'd thought she might eek out a modified version of her original trip. Sleep in the car. Live on crackers or something cheap, then show up back at her airport for her return flight on December 29th. No problem.

No problem, except for now her car was in the drink and she was inching along the side of it, in the dark, with snowflakes soaking into the butt of her jeans.

She reached the edge of the trunk and looked over. To her amazement, the suitcase handle had stretched out and was easily within reach. And not only that, the stream wasn't as deep as she'd feared and there was a path of large rocks—albeit snow-covered—leading from the car to the embankment.

The problem was the embankment. From the glow of her headlights she could see where she'd flown off the road and into a deep ravine. No one would be able to see her car from the road. No one would be stopping to help, even if they were out in that storm.

The wind was gone, like it had just picked up long enough to spin her off the road. But the storm continued in a steady straight fall of snowflakes that enjoyed a little spotlight before disappearing into the water in front of her car. It didn't seem much colder than a snowstorm in Washington State, but at home, she rarely fell into creeks. Her feet were freezing fast; even if the air wasn't cold, the water had been icy. The tingling in her toes had stopped. Now she couldn't feel them at all.

But what a romantic place to die.

She'd come to Scotland to find her old positive attitude again and hopefully a side order of romance. But she could only be positive she was going to die if she didn't get moving.

She pulled her luggage free and pulled it onto the bumper in front of her before she tried to stand. Then she found a good grip with her shoes and willed her frozen toes to hang on tight before she hurled the suitcase as far as she could toward the embankment. It went about five pathetic feet, but didn't sink too far into the snow. The handbag sailed easily to the top of the ridge.

The pins-and-needles feeling returned to her feet. She didn't have any time to be choosey about where she jumped. She just said another quick prayer and pushed off.

An athlete, she was not. The ground came up at her a little fast and a lot hard. Her grunt could have scared off a hungry wolf. But she was grateful not to have landed in water, and even more grateful no one was standing by with camera.

The ground beneath her feet began to slide, but she clawed her way through slushy mud and onto solid ground. The handle of her suitcase was still fully extended, so she was able to pull the bag to her with her icicle fingers without stepping back toward the water. The slide of the car had created a slope, so she was able to drag herself and her things back up to the road. She doubted she could have climbed up the bank any other way considering the way the ridge curved back over the water like an ocean wave just before it crashes.

Except for the fact that she'd spun off the road, she was feeling pretty lucky all around—well, the parts of her that still had feeling. She took a minute to catch her breath and look around. She needed to get her cell phone. If she didn't have reception, it would at least be a light for a while.

The headlights died.

She stood very still.

With no moonlight or starlight coming through the thick cloud cover, an inky blackness surrounded her like a pack of menacing dogs. She couldn't see her hand in front of her face; she held it up and wiggled her fingers just to make sure. If she hadn't been paying attention, just that second before the lights went out, she might have gotten turned around—*she might have walked right back off that ridge!*

Looking for her handbag, and the cell, wasn't worth the risk.

In spite of the pain in her fingers, she dragged her suitcase into the middle of the road so she could keep track of it—not the suitcase, the road. There weren't any headlights, but she wasn't surprised. The last town she'd passed had rolled up its sidewalks hours ago. And she hadn't seen another car since the sun went down. At midnight, it seemed the only thing awake was the snow.

She couldn't see it, of course, but she felt the gentle build of its weight on her shoulders and imagined she could hear the giant flakes landing gently on the ground, like whisper-light rain. The peace of it was incredible. She wondered if her deaf students ever enjoyed that peace, or if it always seemed a curse.

It was going to be the peace of death for her if she didn't find a way to get warm. And since the only thing she had, in the darkness, was a suitcase full of clothes, they would have to do.

She opened that suitcase then squatted down to feel around, to find out what was dry. Unfortunately, frozen fingers weren't capable of differentiating between wet and dry, so she held things up to her neck. Nothing seemed to be wet. She reached inside her coat and, with her hands in her arm pits, she thawed her fingers for a long minute so she could untie her wet shoes. She got them off, along with her wet socks, then stepped onto the dry lid. She hovered over her dry clothes to protect them from the falling snow, but wasn't very successful.

The frozen bottoms of her jeans slapped against her bare feet and made her jump. She tried to unzip her pants, to take them off, but it was too late. Her fingers were frozen. But if the snow didn't stop, whatever she put on would eventually be wet anyway.

Suddenly, she remembered the scissors in the inner pocket. At conferences, she was always running into people who were eager to start signing with their child, so she always kept some print outs of common signs in her bag, and a pair of scissors to cut up the flash cards. It was her idea of a tool kit.

And now it was going to save her life! She could cut off the icy ends of her pant legs and not need to take off her jeans at all.

She found the scissors right where they were supposed to be. Then she began hacking away at the best fitting jeans she'd ever owned, hoping the activity would help to warm her hands, hoping her joints wouldn't freeze up and stop working. She had so little feeling left she wasn't sure if the cloth was cutting or not.

She ignored the urge to lie down and rest.

Finally, one pant leg fell away. There was a little more sensation while she cut into the next one, a little more welcomed pain. Then the other side dropped away. The backs of her jeans were damp, but the warmth from her body would keep the rest from icing up.

A few tortured minutes later, she was wearing everything she'd packed, including two pair of socks for her feet, followed by the red rain boots she should have been wearing in the first place. Around her ears, she tied the pantyhose she'd tossed in, even though there was a hole in one toe. Five pairs of panties protected the top of her head from the ever-falling snow.

In the end, Bree stood inside an empty suitcase—her new safe place—wearing her short coat over a little black sparkly dress, over a plaid flannel nightie, over sweatpants, over her cutoff jeans. Making it impossible to zip up her coat were three shirts and two sweaters. The last two pair of socks went over her hands. After the blood started pumping the way it should, through all her extremities, she found a new reason to want to survive.

She was going to punch that little Scotsman in the nose for handing her the keys to a rental car with no snow tires! She'd never punched anyone in the nose before, but she was pretty sure she could pull it off.

The idea made her warm. In fact, she was getting good and toasty, standing there in the dark, in a suitcase filling up with snow, when she thought she saw a light. Then another. But they didn't act like headlights.

Did Scotland have lightning bugs? Did they have them in winter?

Even as they moved closer—and thank heavens they *were* moving closer—they stayed an equal distance apart. She blinked hard, tried to figure out if it was a panic-induced mirage. She closed her eyes for as long as she could stand, then looked again.

Yes! Lights! Moving her way! She was saved! But she'd huddled there in her suitcase, in the middle of the road, thinking for so long that it was the only safe place to be, that she was reluctant to step out of it.

Blackness still surrounded her. The lights were so small and far away, they only served to show her how complete the darkness was, how vulnerable she'd been to creatures that could probably see well in the darkness if they weren't huddled and asleep in their dens.

With her ears straining for animal noises, it seemed like an hour passed before the lights came closer. But she wasn't stepping out of her zippered life raft until the Coast Guard arrived.

CHAPTER TWO

Bree heard the horses before she realized the lights swaying back and forth were a pair of lanterns hanging on each side of an old-fashioned carriage, shining on the backs of four huge white horses.

She was standing in the very center of the road, so there was no way they could pass without driving over her. She only hoped the driver wasn't asleep at the wheel because she wasn't sure how fast she could move if it came down to it. She waved her arms and gave her best football stadium whistle while she bounced on her legs. With each little jump, pain shot up from her heels to the back of her neck, but at least she was alive to feel it.

"Ho, there!" A man sat high on the front of the vehicle. He was wearing a top hat, of all things, but who was she to complain?

The horses stopped more than ten feet from her and she sighed in relief, not knowing if she could have gotten out of the way fast enough. She still felt glued to the spot as if her life depended on it.

And as that thought bounced around in her head, she got the strangest impression she should keep on standing there and wait for the next car to come along. Like someone was whispering in her ear that she might end up regretting something. A chill ran up her spine, but it only served to remind her how close she'd come to freezing to death, and that was all it took to get her moving.

"Be ye Miss Colby, then?"

She'd just stepped out of the suitcase when the man called out and she seriously considered climbing back in again. How could he know who she was? If he came from the rental place, how did he know she'd spun off the road and not gone on to her destination?

"You know m...m...my name?"

The man jumped down into the slushy road and hurried forward. His hair was gray, nearly white, even. But he didn't look more than fifty or so.

"The name's Ferguson. Sawyer Ferguson. I'm from the HSTC, the Heart of Scotland Tour Company. I'm sorry I failed to meet you at the pub, lass. Uh..." He frowned and looked her over. "Uh. That is... Ye are a *lassie,* underneath all that. Are ye no'?"

Bree looked down at her substantial girth, then back at him and nodded.

"Oh, fine, then. That's fine. You're not quite to order, but that's fine. It'll all work out fine."

He bent down to get her suitcase. But since she was pretty sure she'd just been insulted, she put a boot on the corner to stop him.

He straightened and raised his brows but said nothing.

"What? I'm not quite to order?" She'd be damned if she was going to be unclear about anything else during her week-long vacation. The last thing she'd been unclear about was wanting a car with snow tires.

"Oh, tut-tut," the driver said. "Meant nothing by it a'tall. Just that all the planning in the universe can't guarantee how things will go, is all. I was up on the castle road and saw the car lights take a wee spin. I worried it might be you. No one but a yank would brave this storm in the wee hours, eh? So I came a runnin'. But would ye mind telling me yer full name, so I know I've the right lassie?"

Bree pulled her foot back from the suitcase. "Brianna Catherine Colby. I go by Bree. The rental car is in the water. I need to let someone know."

His smile stretched all the way across his face. It was a little creepy.

"No worries, lass. I'll be happy to make the call, tell them where to find ol' Bess."

"Ol' Bess?"

"Aye. It's the terrible excuse for a car that Ronald Dugan finagled you into this eve. He'll return your money. I'll see to it."

As usual, the return of some of her hard-earned money made her feel better and released a little of the steam she'd been building up on behalf of the car rental man. Unfortunately, that was all that was keeping her warm. A shiver rolled through her body and one of her panties slipped past the pantyhose and down over one eye. Mr. Ferguson started laughing.

"'Tis very creative, the way you kept yerself warm, lass. But I promise you'll be nice and cozy inside the carriage." A horse moved a bit and the light of the lantern shined on her handbag. "Oh, I'll collect that, Miss Colby. Not to worry."

She headed for the carriage, but she wasn't about to stop worrying. She'd already been the victim of one old Scotsman that night, and she wasn't about to trust the next one in line. But survival came first. Tomorrow was soon enough to make heads roll.

The carriage wheels had been changed out for rails. "It's a sleigh," she said. "I've been saved by Santa Claus."

The old man choked and gave her a frown. "'Tis a coach, make no mistake, lass. Nice and warm inside." He opened the door. "Up ye go then."

There was even a lantern inside, and whether or not it was a fire hazard, it was probably what was keeping the interior warm. Ferguson gave her a hand up. She found the bench under a thick blanket that felt like lamb's wool. And she wasn't sure if it was because of the many layers of clothes she wore, or the stuffing, but the seat felt like a cloud. She was tempted to lie down on it.

The man reached across her to tuck in the blanket and she reached out and grabbed his arm.

"I'd have died if you hadn't come along, Mr. Ferguson. I mean, actually *died*. So, thank you." She yawned. "Maybe I can do a better job of thanking you when my shock wears off."

"Rest yerself, lass. In the time it takes to pull this carriage back up to the castle, you can have yourself a nice wee nap. Forget your troubles. We'll just leave them in the drink, along with Ol' Bess. What say ye?"

"Sure." That was all the sense she was capable of since her mind kept catching on the word castle. "Um, did you say castle?"

"Aye. We'll head there straight away. It's a little surprise, y' see. When I meet our travelers at the pub, I give them the news that they won't be stayin' in a Bed and Breakfast after all, but a castle the first night. Most folks are tickled, o' course. I think it a grand place to begin your tour of the Heart of Scotland. And the beds are comfortable to boot. Lovely goose down. I can honestly say they don't make them like that anymore, more's the pity." He closed the carriage door and a few seconds later, the carriage lurched forward.

She leaned back but doubted she'd be able to sleep. Her adrenal glands were running overtime and she wasn't quite ready to appreciate the fact that her tour of Scotland was back on track. She needed a big fire and a warm bed, maybe in the morning she'd be able to digest everything that had happened in the last few hours.

She *had* been driving for hours. But if so, even at a snail's pace, how could the guy be stumbling onto her so far away from Burnshire? Unless she'd been going in circles...

The jingle of chains sounded like sleigh bells, and she wondered why the man had been so offended she'd called his vehicle a sleigh. Maybe he just resented being called Santa Claus.

After a bump and a slip sideways, she gathered her blanket close and wondered if she could make it into a dress if she suddenly found herself soaked again. Of course, she'd need scissors. The silly image made her smile, and she started to relax to a slow and steady rhythm.

Clop. Clop. Whoosh. Jingle.

Clop. Clop. Whoosh. Jingle.

Adding to that rhythm was the sound of the coachman's voice warming up a tune. It was as if he was singing just above her head. Not a Christmas song. More like a dirge—slow and low and melancholy—a lonely kind of song that makes you wonder at the depth of the singer's sadness, but it enchants you just the same.

He hummed an entire melody, then started again with words.

Let not yer cries...call down the moon.
Let not yer prayers...be led astray.
I' the coachman's guise, he'll grant yer boon,
And ye shall rue...the price ye pay.

Take back the breath... Take back the sigh.
Give not yer name... Yer boon deny.
The Foolish Fire...comes not in twain.
'Tis the coachman's lanterns
Come for ye.

With hands of white...and horses matched.
He'll guide thy love...to broken heart.
Of measured dreams...he'll grant behalf.
And take from thee...e'en the beggar's part.

Then he hummed the chorus once more. Bree was intrigued by the obviously old-fashioned tune, but she couldn't stay awake. The warmth was seeping into her bones and her blinks were stretching longer and longer. Finally, she closed her eyes and concentrated on the words, wishing she'd be able to remember even a line or two.

He'll calm the hounds... The wind he'll wield
When the Moon he walks...'mong beasts and man.
So be still yer hopes... Trust not the yield
'Til the hounds behowl...the night again.

Again, the coachman hummed and Bree struggled to hold on, to see if there might be another verse, if maybe there could be a happy ending, somehow.

Then her thoughts slid into a comfortable, inky blackness.

CHAPTER THREE

———————⊹⊱✾⊰⊹———————

Heathcliff barred the window against the wind and quit the tower room. He'd find no answers there. As he passed the child's room, he could not help but peek inside, to assure himself she fared well. His heart stopped when he spied the covers pushed aside, but it started again when he found her at the window, no doubt looking for the self-same moon to which he'd addressed his pleas but a wee while ago.

Her golden hair glowed in the candlelight, as if the moon now hid behind the strands.

Blond hair. So different from his own black mane. But he'd heard of children's hair turning darker as they grew. It meant nothing.

Whatever she saw in the storm clouds seemed to make her happy, and she turned her smile on him. Awkwardly, he reached out, placed his hand on her head, and gave her a careful pat.

"I'm sorry, lassie. Your nurse had to leave us for a wee while. 'Twill be but the pair of us to fend for ourselves for a few days."

Her little hand snaked its way into his and she squeezed, as if sensing he needed comfort more than she.

"We'll be fine, cherub. Just fine."

Once he'd banked her fire and tucked the wee lass beneath her heavy covers, he had to pull the drapes to coax her eyes to close and prevent her from watching out the window. He was afraid that whatever it was she wished for, she was not going to get.

There was no need to start yet another fire, so instead of retiring to his study, he returned to the parlor where glowing coals awaited another bit of wood. Once there, however, he doubted the chill in his bones had aught to do with the storm and forbore tossing on another log. He poured himself a whiskey, hoping the burn of it might reach that deep chill, but his hand stopped before the glass reached his lips.

Should a father drink spirits with a child in his sole care?

He set the glass aside and scrubbed his face with both hands. Neither should he sleep, he thought, just in case he was needed. After all, the delicate cherub might not be able to rouse him from a deep slumber. Perhaps he should have given her a large bell. Perhaps he should have arranged a pallet for her there, in the parlor, so she would not need to look far to find him. But that was nonsense. She wasn't a puppy, she was a lass. She needed a bed, did she not?

Dear lord, he was going to go mad trying to learn this fathering business on his own.

He forced himself to calm, to sit and watch the flames that popped up in defiance of the dying embers. He imagined slumber overtaking the wee lassie and lulling her troubles away with a silent flute. Sleep was no doubt a precious boon for one who'd just been abandoned to a man supposed to be her father. Surely the girl would have nightmares this eve, with her nurse having fled. The rumors from the village likely scared the woman off, for who would wish to be pent up with the grandson of a Muir Witch, laird or no? Christmas was a holy holiday, not one to be spent near one rumored to dance with the devil.

He had to own the wee lass had done well thus far. She was quick with a smile, no matter the news he gave her. A lovely sweet charge no right-minded nurse would abandoned into a strange man's hands.

Again, he remembered bending down to greet the child, and when he'd stood once more, the woman was gone. He might have chased her to ground and bribed her to confess all—heaven knew he had coin to spare—but there had been none to watch after the child. And how could he have left the wee lassie alone?

Silence settled in his mind. A coal shattered under the weight of another and sparks escaped and fled up the chimney. A flame roused, then worried itself to death over a stick too green yet to burn.

Could she be mine?

For the hundredth time that day, he thought back six, seven, eight years, trying to remember a woman he'd loved, a face he recalled with fondness, but there was no one. Eight years ago, he'd been as lonely as he was now. But oh, how he wished she was his. How he wished there might be something of himself to carry on once he was laid low in the kirkyard. How he wished he'd found someone to woo and wed before the reputation of his grandmother and her twin sister ruined his own. Someone who cared not for the color of his coin.

Could he buy a wife? Certainly. But he'd never want a wife that could be bought. Better to have no children at all, than give them such a mother.

He determined to make sense of this new predicament. If it meant proving the child was sired by another, no matter. After the New Year, he would hunt down the nurse and have the truth. By then, the wee lassie might well choose to stay with him in any case.

Perhaps he could find a way to make her the daughter of his heart.

A ruckus stirred at the front of the house and he rushed to the entryway to make certain the noise would cease before it could wake his would-be daughter.

He flung the door wide, just as an older man reached for the knocker.

"Are you mad?" Heathcliff whispered harshly. "There is a wee lass above stairs trying to sleep. I'll not have ye wake her!"

The man bowed and turned his top hat in his hands. "Beg yer pardon, yer lairdship. I've got a lass here as well. Miss Brianna Colby. You've been expecting her I think." The man winked and moved back.

Heathcliff was about to insist that he was expecting no one when he caught sight of the sturdy lass who stumbled forward with a shove from behind. His denial died on his tongue, leaving him temporarily unable to speak.

She was stout, to be sure. And given that she was a woman, she might have proven helpful considering his current dilemma. After all, he'd sent his staff away to spend the holidays with their families, not knowing he'd have a wee lassie to care for. But this woman would not do. No matter the pleasant look of her face, the woman was daft and clearly so, what with the hats she wore on her head. And not just one; he saw at least three brightly colored things perched there, possibly four. And not only were they inappropriate for the current weather, they were defective as well, sporting large holes, every last one of them. It was a fact the hats failed so completely, her fair hair was near to dark with the wet of the snow.

Even if he could see past her daft hats, she had tied silk stockings about her head, perchance to keep her ears warm, as if she did not know they were meant for a woman's legs. But from the look of her, perhaps her legs were far too large for the stockings to fit. Poor thing.

But he had enough to worry over with the child. He would not take on another responsibility and this one with perhaps a broken mind. Why, he would never be able to allow her near the bairn!

"Nay." His tone offered no invitation to argue.

The woman frowned at him, confused.

"Nay," he said again, looking pointedly at her head.

Her eyes flew wide and both hands made quick work of the odd hats and stockings. She hid them behind her back and blushed a deeper shade of red beneath her cold cheeks.

"I crashed into the water," she said. "I came very close to freezing to death. I promise you I'm not an idiot. And I don't usually go around with underwear on the top of my head."

Underthings? Truly?

He took his imagination in hand and concentrated on other details. Her speech was strange. Clearly foreign. She looked past him, trying to peek inside his home, and his heart tripped. Had he just been presented with a pair of thieves?

The lass turned about her, no doubt looking for her cohort's support with her storytelling, but the man had scurried away. When she gave Heathcliff her back, he took advantage.

"Away with ye now," he said, then shut the door. She would have no choice but to get back in her carriage and move on to the next town.

"Wait!" Her cry was barely discernible though the heavy oak, but again, he was forced to open it, to stop her from waking the child.

"Shh!" He gave her his fiercest frown. "Madame. Ye will climb back into yer..."

But the carriage was gone.

She pointed to the place it had been only a moment before. "He left me! He just...left me," she repeated. "I didn't even hear him go!"

It had to be a ruse to ensure she got inside the castle. No doubt the man would be back in the wee hours of the night to help her load up what booty she might pilfer whilst the household slept. It gave him only a moment's pause that he, too, had taken no notice when the four-in-hand had departed. And there were no tracks by which to judge, thanks to snow falling even heavier now than when he'd first opened the door.

"Please, sir. Can I just come in and get warm? And use your phone? There has to be someone willing to come get me and take me to a hotel."

Ah, she had a clever tongue. He knew not what a phone was, but there was only one Inn in the village and she likely had passed it on her way up the hill. She needed only lie down on the road and slide her way back. She looked to have enough heft to keep her warm along the way. And even if she was of sound mind, he'd not allow a sneak thief near any child, his or not.

"I've a child in the house, madam. I'll not allow a woman of yer sort around a child. Now be on yer way. There is an Inn at the bottom of the hill, as I'm certain ye know. If ye but stumble and fall, ye will find yourself very near its door. No doubt yer coachman awaits ye there."

Her mouth dropped open and lingered while he stepped back to shut the door again. But it struck something—an odd red boot stuck just inside. Worrying he might have harmed the woman, he opened the door yet again and found genuine worry on her brow. She gave no attention to her foot. At least he'd not caused her pain.

"Please. I'll die out here. I'm not the type to beg, but I'm begging you now. Please. I have to get warm. I nearly froze to death once tonight, and I'm absolutely sure I'll end up a popsicle on your doorstep if you leave me out here."

Popsicle sounded ominous. And despite his sure knowledge that she was up to mischief, he could not assign the shake of her form to acting. The lass was freezing, no question now. If her coachman showed his face again, Heathcliff would see to it the man paid for putting a woman's life in such jeopardy, no matter her character.

He tried to ignore the fact that by closing his door against her, he'd done the same.

"With all the opening and closing, I've likely fanned all the heat from the castle, but ye are welcome to what is left of it." His speech was a bit gruff, but she need not know that he was unhappy with himself more than her.

He was a gentleman and a Scotsman, but betimes he couldna manage both at the same time. At the moment, he was simply a Scot learning how to protect his new child, albeit a half-grown one.

She gave a little thank you as she hurried past him and into his home. Once he'd secured the door, he turned to find her shaking in an altogether new manner.

"Come with me," he said, then took up the candle and led her down the corridor to the garderobe. She clearly needed to relieve herself and might have suffered an accident had she been forced to wait any longer. He placed the candle inside the door and stepped back, but he would not go far. As she closed herself inside the tiny room, she was enjoying the only privacy she'd be allowed while beneath his roof , and as soon as she was able, out the door she'd go.

Nothing was important but the child's safety and whether or not he was imagining things, he felt it best the child not be exposed to his questionable guest.

He shuffled his feet on the stone floor to mask the rustling sounds the woman made. Truly, he'd never before stood about listening to a woman performing her necessaries, and it took a bit of creative shuffling to keep his imagination from joining in. However, when the lass began greeting, even quietly, he panicked and hurried back to the parlor. Better to lose a few baubles to sticky fingers and be done. Dear Lord, but he was no help to a weepin' woman.

CHAPTER FOUR

Bree hoped the rest of Scotland had indoor plumbing! Of course she was in a castle and maybe running pipes might be something the owners couldn't afford, but the bathroom was just a step up from an outhouse, really. She wouldn't complain, though. Her bladder had thawed out with her first lungful of warm air and she'd needed the closest bathroom possible. Thankfully, the potty jig was internationally understood and he'd acted quickly. If she'd been wearing just one more layer of clothing...

After her most desperate need was taken care of, however, the insanity of the situation hit her and she'd fallen apart. She was lucky she wasn't dead. *Very* lucky she wasn't *very* dead. And it looked like the nightmare wasn't over yet! She'd been dumped on someone's doorstep who didn't want her in his home, and if she pissed the guy off, he was grumpy enough to kick her out into the cold again! She didn't have a nice safe car in which she could set up camp. She didn't even know where she was, exactly—only that she had to still be in Scotland or Laird Gorgeous wouldn't have had such a lovely brogue.

But ye are welcome to what's left of it.

She'd tried to cry quietly, since he'd been just outside the doorway. In the end, though, she must have scared him away, since the hall was empty when she came out.

Bree followed the warmth into a living room just off the vaulted entryway. The ceiling was lower there and the heat from the ornate fireplace filled the room. Of course she'd never been in a castle before. She planned to visit lots of them before she had to take her return flight home. But right then, survival was a little more important than chandeliers, mahogany walls, and carved staircases. But just barely. Hopefully, she'd get a chance to appreciate all of it before Laird Gorgeous kicked her to the curb—probably first thing in the morning.

Hopefully, not before then.

She promised herself she wouldn't say something stupid that might piss him off, but the guy was strung a little tight. Who knew what might upset him? Hurrying over to the fireplace and dropping to her knees bought her a little time for the swelling to come down in her face. Her hands were warming up nicely, but he didn't need to know that. Maybe the colder she looked, the longer he'd let her stay. Her nap in the carriage had been toasty, but the second she'd been in the open air again, it seemed like the temperature was half as warm as it had been when she'd done her little fashion show in the middle of the road.

There were plenty of coals, but the pile was meager. The guy was probably on a tight budget, trying to keep his castle open and running. And until she'd arrived, he'd probably only needed to warm himself. But he'd said there was a child there too.

"You said you have a child, trying to sleep?"

He just frowned, like he was telling her to mind her own business. He probably hated Americans or something, and she didn't want to make it worse, so she thought she'd better explain herself.

"I just wondered why the kid isn't in here, if this is the warmest room, you know?"

His frown slowly morphed into horror. "Think ye she is cold? I had not considered!" And with that, he ran from the room.

The look on his face made Bree sick to her stomach. Had he left his child somewhere cold? What kind of man did that? She ran out into the hall and listened for his footsteps.

Upstairs!

She followed quickly, trying not to imagine the worst, trying to enjoy the beautiful piece of wood used for the banister without slowing down. Pins and needles pricked at her feet again, but she took that as a good sign they wouldn't need to be cut off or something. A little while before, she hadn't been so sure.

She found him kneeling by the side of a bed pressing the back of his hand to a pale little forehead framed by blond braids. Or maybe she only looked pale—a single candle next to the bed caused more shadows than light. He clutched a little hand in his and patted it.

"Cherub? Cherub. Can ye hear me, Cherub?" He looked over his shoulder, his eyes pleading with Bree to help him.

How could she refuse? It wasn't like *Mrs*. Gorgeous was around, and Bree did work with children on a daily basis. She hurried to the bed and he shuffled to the side to give her room. She touched the little forehead and her heart lurched. The little girl was cold. *Cold* cold.

"Maybe it's just her exposed skin," Bree said. "It's not like the room is as cold as it is outside, right?" She patted the icy little face.

A giant lump rose in her throat, but she just kept talking, to keep everybody calm. Colbys did not panic.

"Has she been ill? Has she been eating? Drinking?" Bree couldn't resist any longer. To check for a pulse, she pressed her fingers to the little neck no bigger around than her forearm. She didn't think the little thing was breathing.

Two big blue eyes fluttered open and the child gave her a big smile. Her dad gasped, then pushed Bree aside and scooped the girl into his arms, blankets and all. She was pretty sure he was crying when she followed him from the room. She was close to tears, too. It had been an emotionally exhausting day.

A minute later, they were back in the sitting room. He laid the little form on a green velvet chaise lounge that looked like a Chippendale couch with a back and an arm on only one end. He tucked the girl's blankets around her and then he picked up the furniture as if it and its passenger weighed nothing. He carried it closer to the fire and set it down. After he made sure the kid was smiling, Laird Gorgeous started tossing logs on the fire as if he didn't care what it did to his budget. Only when the fire crackled and popped, did he notice Bree again.

"I thought she would need only blankets to keep warm." He reached out and touched the child's forehead again, then he grinned. "Better." His gaze raised to Bree's. "Thank ye."

"No problem," she said. But inside, she was jelly.

If he ever found a reason to smile at her that way, she'd follow him around like a puppy for the rest of her vacation. She might not return home with a lot of souvenirs, but she'd have one helluva happy thought in her pocket.

She thought about complimenting him on his costume, but that might be an insult if his frilly white necktie (or was that part of his shirt?) and tall boots were his idea of fashion.

"Where is her mom?"

He just shook his head.

She decided the woman must be either dead or blind if she wasn't standing on the battlements to keep other women away from *him*. He was at least six four, maybe taller. She remembered how he'd filled up the doorway when the coachman had pushed her from behind. She was lucky he was busy staring at the underwear on her head so he hadn't notice her staring—and panting—in his face.

His shoulders looked twice as wide as hers—the kind of guy that makes a girl feel small and vulnerable. His eyes were dark, his brows even darker, and his messy black hair went way past his shoulders. His face was the kind that belonged to quarterbacks and class presidents. The kind of guy that never noticed she was alive. And while he was busy not noticing her, she sucked up the sight of him like a girl dying of thirst, forced to drink through a straw.

His jaw was square, but the left corner was sharper than the other, like he'd had the right edge worn down by too many fist fights. And he was noticing her noticing.

Crap!

His look felt like he'd reached out and touched her face. A little chill ran up her spine and into her hair as she bent down next to the chaise, both to speak to the child and get her imagination under control.

"What's your name?" Bree asked.

The girl just smiled.

"She doesna speak," the man said.

Bree took a deep breath while that old feeling poured over her, through her, around her, but this time, it had nothing to do with the Scotsman. It had been a while since she'd felt it—the absolute rightness about the path she'd chosen for her life. If she was honest, she hadn't felt it since she'd started dating David, the guy who always made her feel like she should be doing something else, something *he* might approve of, something that would make him look at her as if she was finally worthy of his interest.

She couldn't believe she'd had to travel all the way to Scotland to feel it again.

Bree smiled at the girl. "Can you hear?" she asked.

The girl nodded. Bree patted her cheek and walked to the other side of the room, nodding for Laird Gorgeous to follow her. She was almost surprised when he did.

"Was she born mute? Or is it something else? Vocal chords?" Bree kept her voice low.

She'd crossed a line again. He was back to frowning at her.

Finally, he shook his head. "I know not."

Okay, that was just messed up. What kind of doctors did they have in the Highlands, if they couldn't even tell a guy why his daughter couldn't speak?

"What do ye ken of vocal chords?" he asked.

"Kin?" She didn't understand the word.

"Ken. To know. What does your sort know of vocal chords?"

He'd called her a sneak thief before. Apparently he hadn't changed his mind about her. But she really couldn't blame him. Everything that had happened to her that day was just insane, and if she was smart, she'd be suspecting everyone else's motives too, including those of Laird Gorgeous. But she wasn't feeling particularly smart at the moment, just a little emotional.

"Ever heard of American Sign Language? I teach deaf and mute children, okay? I'm not a sneak thief, whatever that means. I'm not a spy. I'm not some family services chick trying to catch you being a bad father." Although, if she had been, he'd have been in trouble. "I teach children how to speak with their hands, sometimes with their actual voices. And I teach parents how to do the same. So cut me some slack. Move the couch back a little so your daughter doesn't catch on fire, and try to be nice."

He'd thanked her, right? He wouldn't throw her out now, just because she was a little worn out and a little cranky. But then again, there was that American thing. For all she knew he'd toss her butt out just because she was a yank. The carriage driver wasn't the only one to have called her that since her plane had landed.

All of a sudden, the man started chuckling. It was impossible for Bree not to smile at the deep rumble of it. He'd found something funny, and she was afraid Bree Colby was that something. But even if he was laughing at her expense, she couldn't very well march out his door in a huff, could she?

Then the chuckling opened up into loud laughter.

The girl was peeking over the back of the chaise. She was enjoying the sound too.

"Who sent you, madam?" He gasped for another breath. "The Man in the Moon? For I swear to you, I was just laying my complaints at his feet, promising all I have if he would only send someone to me who could help me speak with my new daughter."

She stopped smiling. A tune flooded back into her head, and a little dirge about making deals with the moon. It was all just a little too eerie for her. And there had been a warning. What was the warning? About not liking the price or something? Something depressing, she was sure. In fact, apart from laying eyes on Laird Gorgeous, this whole day was a little too depressing for her taste, and she wasn't going to face any more of it while standing on her feet.

As it turned out, her knees had been eavesdropping on her thoughts and took matters into their own hands. She watched as the floor started coming at her in slow motion. But then Laird Gorgeous was there, scooping her up, just like he'd done with his little girl.

He frowned again, then tossed her in the air and caught her again. The little girl clapped her hands, clearly enjoying the show. Bree tried to push away, but he squeezed her tight.

"You don't weigh as much as I suspected, lass. Have you not eaten well? Would you like some food? Some mulled wine?"

"I'll skip the wine, but I could eat. Apparently I'm not thinking too clearly, so the food would help; the wine would not." She looked at his neck. It was much safer than looking at his lips, she thought, considering his little girl was watching, and she had yet to hear why his wife was not around. "Um. You can put me down now."

He just grunted and put her on the chaise with his daughter.

"Stay put, mind ye," he said and headed for the hallway. Then he turned back, as if he couldn't stand to leave. He looked embarrassed, but took a deep breath and asked, "Ye've nae come to...steal away the child, have ye?"

CHAPTER FIVE

The question was poor form, but Heathcliff could not seem to leave the room without being certain the wee bairn was safe with the strange woman. The incredulous look on her face was answer enough, though, so he turned on his heel and hurried away, to find something in the kitchens for the three of them. It was well past midnight, but it did not seem as though any of them were ready for sleep just yet. And in case the Man in the Moon decided to add another to their little gathering, they'd all need a bite or two to sustain them.

Man in the Moon, indeed.

After what he'd just learned, naught should surprise him. And fear of yet another surprise had led him to ask such a bold question. He could not bear to return to the parlor and find the pair of them gone. It might just lay him low.

The cheese was a bit dry, but the bread was fresh. And although the apple pie had been left for his Christmas supper, he imagined tonight would be a better time to celebrate. What was a holiday when compared with the wee lass being rescued from his neglect?

A shiver rolled through him when he remembered the feel of her cold hand in his. He'd never felt such on a person who yet lived. But perhaps children were different, turning cold as quickly as they warmed. He would just have to keep her with him at all times until she was big enough to make her own heat, that was all.

He prepared enough mulled wine for two, enough buttermilk for three, then put it all on a heavy tray with the food and hurried back to the parlor. He stopped short, however, when he realized he'd interrupted.

The woman was stripping off her clothes before the fire. The child watched in wonder, but he doubted the look on his face was quite the same.

Her coat was draped around the shoulders of a chair. Her strange red boots sat together on the floor, the firelight glancing across their surface made it appear as if they were made of glass. Upon the seat lay the neatly folded black tunic that sparkled as if covered in stars. What strange clothes they wore in America. The tartan gown she was currently lifting off her head was of poor quality; he could nearly see through the plaid material.

But alas, she was still wearing breeches beneath— not that he'd wished otherwise, of course. It would not do, after all, to have the younger lass believe that stripping oneself bare was appropriate behavior for the parlor.

He took a moment to be pleased over his new fatherly attitude. Perhaps he might be a passable guardian after all. If he could only keep the cherub alive. She was like some wee lamb that needed him to watch over her as she grew—and likely to keep the wolves away once she was full-grown.

He shook his head, disgusted with himself, standing there judging other wolves while he himself watched a woman remove her clothes.

There were a surprising lot of them and she was growing leaner by the moment. And younger as well.

He only watched with one eye as she removed one sweater, then another. A rather over-large shirt came off next. But when she bent to push a pair of odd gray breeches from her legs, he closed his eyes completely. Unfortunately, the hour had weakened his will and his eyes flew open again of their own accord, only to find she wore yet another pair of breeches. Only the last were cut off just at the knee. Between that point and the tops of her sadly short stockings, her legs were bare for all and sundry to see!

Finally, it looked as if she had removed all she was going to, though he waited a moment to be sure. Then he cleared his throat in case she meant to cover her legs before he walked fully into the room. Instead, she sat to one side of the cherub, which left room for him on the opposite side. At the moment, he thought it might be wiser to go sit outside in the snow than to sit so close to the pile of clothes so recently wrapped around the woman's body. For she was, indeed a woman, though much younger and more fit than he could have imagined beneath all that cloth.

Indeed, since the distraction of her substantial girth had been removed, he was better able to appreciate how lovely was Miss Brianna Colby. Her expressive blue eyes caught him staring and she blushed. The fire had dried her hair to a fairy blond, which looked even whiter next to the pink of her skin.

Silently, he sent the Man in the Moon a begrudging *thank you*. Aloud, he asked, "Were ye wearing everything you have, lass?" He placed the tray on a small table and moved it all in front of the fire before taking the seat open to him.

She laughed. It was an honest laugh, not like the ladies at court who flirted freely with him and would wed his money and titles without a thought to his grandmother's reputation. He wondered how much of this one's story had been as honest as her laugh.

"I was wearing everything I could find in my suitcase, actually. If I could have figured out how to wear the suitcase, I probably would have tried that too."

"A *suit* case? Some sort of luggage?"

She gave him a narrow look. "You've never heard of suitcases? I don't think so."

"I would like to see this thing."

"Even if I believed you've never seen a suitcase, I don't think the driver left it. I can't believe he left *me*. I'm going to make sure he gets in trouble for screwing up so badly. If he had picked me up at the station, I would have never had to rent that car, so I wouldn't have slid off the road into the water. I would have never..."

The woman paused as if suddenly mired in thought. But then her countenance changed. She looked down at the lassie and smiled.

"But then I would have never met this little pumpkin."

His eyes met hers over the wee one's head, but the woman quickly looked away. Would that she were as happy to have met him. But still, it was kind of her to consider how her little rant affected the child. A motherly instinct to be sure. And wouldn't the cherub be needing a mother?

He shook his head. The woman was clearly not meant for him. He was appalled he'd even imagined such a thing. It would be foolish to harbor more such thoughts until he'd had a few hours' sleep.

He pulled the small table closer and began serving. The child looked at the pie and wrinkled her nose, but took a large piece of cheese and a slice of bread. The way she relished her food, for the third time that day, made him wonder if she'd ever had much to eat before arriving on his stoop. He tried to coax her into eating just a bite of pie, then lifted the fork to the woman's mouth, giving her no choice but to take what he offered. She choked, but whether she choked on the pie or the rush of blood to her face, he could not tell.

He was surprised when he felt that same rush. He'd clearly gone mad.

"Look, lassie," he said. "Miss Colby likes the pie. If ye want to grow up to be as pretty, ye must eat more than just cheese and bread.

Too late, he heard the words he'd allowed out of his mouth. Good lord! But his madness was forgotten when the wee lassie dropped open her gob eager for a bite of pie. Perhaps he would make a right clever father after all. After she swallowed, she jumped up to look at her face in a small mirror set low on the wall, and he and Miss Colby burst into laughter.

"She must think the pie works right quickly," he whispered.

"Magic pie," the woman whispered back. "Or else she's never seen her face in a mirror before. How old is she?"

It was a simple question, but he was afraid to tell her the truth, afraid he'd be found lacking and the child would be taken away. For some reason, he felt this stranger had the power to hurt him that much, even if she had not the inclination. And if he'd learned anything at all from his oddly talented grandmother, it was to be mindful of forebodings.

"What is it?" she asked and placed a hand on his forearm. "Maybe you would rather I mind my own business, but there might be some way for me to help you. For some reason I landed on your doorstep tonight. And if it happened for a reason, then I want to help you."

He searched her eyes and found only honesty looking back at him. Well, honesty, and perhaps a little interest. Her gaze kept dropping to his neck for some reason. Had he lost a button?

"I surrender," he said, and sat back with a sigh. "A woman brought her to my door only this morning. She claimed the child was mine now, and that the girl did not speak. I was so surprised. Mind ye, the child canna be mine in truth, but while I crouched to take a good look at her and to assure her she was safe here, the nurse slipped away. I could not run after her without leaving the child on her own." He explained how he'd sent the servants off to their families for the holidays. He and the child had been quite alone and unable to carry on much of a conversation, until Brianna Colby had pushed her way into the castle.

"You're not married then? No Mrs... Uh..."

"Heathcliff, Laird McKinnon, at your service. There is no Lady McKinnon." It may have been the first time in his adult life when the confession sounded like good news to his ears.

"Heathcliff? That's your first name?" She looked as if she might burst out laughing. At least she'd gotten used to looking at him without blushing—for the most part. He had that effect on many a lass, for all the good it did him once they discovered who he was.

"My given name, yes. You find it amusing for some reason?"

"I'm sorry. I'm sure you get teased all the time about Wuthering Heights. It's just that my middle name is Catherine."

He felt as though he'd been saying as much all the long day, but he said it again. "I doona understand."

She rolled her lovely eyes. "You don't know Wuthering Heights? I thought every British kid had to know the classics."

"Classics?"

She gave him a kindly smile that made him feel like a simple child. Though he liked the smile, he cared not for the feeling.

"Books. Wuthering Heights is my favorite, written by Emily Bronte. Published in 1847, I think. Maybe '48. I've read it dozens of times."

His blood ran cold, pushing a chill to every extreme of his body. His grandmother's voice rang in his ears. *When a Muir gets a feeling, everyone best keep on their toes.* Though he was only one quarter Muir, there was enough in his blood to make the townsfolk leery of him. Perhaps they were justified in their suspicions after all. For his chill tasted of something else as well and whispered in his head...

Something wicked this way comes.

"Do you have this book with ye, lass?" He tried his damnedest to appear casual.

She frowned and rolled those eyes once again. "It's not like I carry a copy with me when I go on vacation. But I can tell you the story."

"I'd rather ye tell me that date again. When did ye say it was published?"

"1847. I think. I could be wrong, but it's somewhere around there."

"Nay, lass. Ye're mistaken. Surely ye meant to say 1747."

She shook her head. "No. I'm sure it was mid-*nineteenth* century. Victorian era."

"*Victorian* era? Mid-nineteenth century? Just what year do ye suppose it is now?"

"Uh, twenty twelve."

She gave him that indulgent smile again and he most definitely did not like it. In fact, it was best he not appreciate anything about the woman since she was obviously mad. No matter what she'd said about wearing her underthings to protect her hair, the woman was not right in the head. And if his doorstep continued to be as busy on the morrow, his family castle would be a lunatic asylum by New Year's Day.

No matter how she might help him learn to speak with the child, he would get the daft young woman on her way in the morning, to get her good and far from his young charge. God, or Fate, had gotten it wrong. Sending Brianna Colby to his door was not going to solve his problems. And since even the bloody Man in the Moon hadn't come to his aid, it might be best if he stopped answering his door altogether.

Someone slammed the knocker on the front door. Then they slammed it again. And again. The sound resembled that of a blacksmith striking his anvil.

On another day it might have been amusing to have his thought interrupted by such banging. But not this day, for he was certain *Something Wicked...*

...had arrived.

CHAPTER SIX

As Heathcliff reached for the doorknob, hairs arose on the nape of his neck. But he was no coward. Not answering his door had been a silly notion. Of course he would open it and deal with whomever stood upon his stoop.

He ignored the fact that he was unable to breathe while he swung the door wide, but there was no one there. At his feet was a strange square box covered with green cloth. A missive was perched upon it, growing soggy under a covering of snowflakes that sparkled as they melted.

He place the missive between his teeth and lifted the box, nearly falling backward when it turned out to be so much lighter than expected—quite like his latest guest.

Was this her luggage? Had the coachman come again? He must still be lurking nearby since the knocking had stopped when he was but a few steps from the door.

A moment later, with a lantern in hand, Heathcliff ran out into the darkness, searching for the coachman's footprints in the snow, or whatever person might have delivered the green box. He stomped to the steps that led to the ruins of the ancient wall walk and, holding his lantern high, looked over the road that led down the hill. Nothing. Not so much as a hoof print was visible.

A sudden wind pushed at him, sent snowflakes to dance around his lantern, urged him to retreat from the wall before he lost his balance.

"The snow has but drifted over the tracks, that is all," he murmured and went back inside. By the time he stepped back inside, he believed it.

The wee lass was asleep with her head in the lap of the madwoman. The latter looked at him expectantly.

"Where did you go?" she asked.

"Someone left this box at the door. A rabbit, I would suspect, for as quickly as they got away. I caught sight of no one." He came to stand before her and thanks to a small handle, he was able to pull the case from behind his back.

"My suitcase!" Her face lit with excitement, but she paused to move out from under the child and beckoned him away from the sleeping bairn. "It had to have been that man."

"The coachman?"

"Yes. Who else would have it? Who else would know where I was?"

"I thought the same." He thought some other things as well, but was not yet ready to share them.

She performed some strange ritual around the edges of the box and the top lifted away. She then showed him how she'd used the flap to keep her feet dry while she donned all her clothing. Heathcliff could not help but laugh.

How could this sharp-witted woman also be so daft?

"You stopped smiling. What's wrong?"

He shook his head. "Ye puzzle me, is all. Ye seem so clever, and yet ye know not the current year. But I wonder, do ye measure the years differently in America?"

"What? I'm sorry. I don't understand the question." She collapsed onto one Queen Anne chair and he sank onto the other.

"I only know that today is the twenty third of December in the year eighteen hundred six, and ye claim the year is twenty-twelve."

She laughed. "Very funny. Eighteen oh six. Is that supposed to explain why you don't have a phone and you don't know what a suitcase is? That I've somehow traveled through time to teach you and the girl how to use sign language?" She laughed again, but looked a mite worried.

His stomach lurched, but he ignored it and said lightly, "When one is rumored to have witches in the family, 'tis fair foolish to speculate in such a way. To do so is to invite...mischief."

"What? Wait. Witches? You have witches in your family?" She sat up a bit straighter and looked a bit too excited by the prospect for his liking.

"My grandmother was rumored to be such. She merely had odd...talents." And he missed her dearly.

"What kind of odd talents? Please tell me she didn't have a talent for time travel."

Truth be told, he might suspect as much, as his grandmother had claimed many a strange thing would happen in the future. He knew not how she acquired her knowledge, or if she merely suffered from wild imaginings.

He suddenly remembered the missive and retrieved it from the entryway. The envelope was quite soggy. He hoped the message was still legible.

"This was left with yer luggage."

"Probably an apology for taking off with my bag in the first place. And he still has my purse, with my airline ticket, my credit cards, and my passport. But why give me back the suitcase and not my handbag? If he's going to take off with my passport and airline ticket, why risk bringing me an empty suitcase? It just doesn't make sense."

"These are valuables he has taken?"

She sighed. "You're kidding, right? I can't get back home without them. I can't fly. I can't buy food. I can't prove who I am." She stood and began to pace, but stopped. "I can at least cancel my credit cards if you have the internet."

He walked quietly to the other side of the room and sat the envelope on the little table before the fire for the time being, afraid it might fall apart in his hands if he tried to open it before it dried. Not wishing her to read too much on his face, he spoke to her while looking into the fire.

"I am truly sorry I do not have these things ye need. We shall just have to wait for the storm to end before we can do aught to solve yer dilemmas."

Her gasp forced him to turn.

"It's the twenty-first century, for hellsakes. They're giving iPads to children in Africa, and you don't even have the *internet?* This guy can take every penny I have if he knows what he's doing. Holy crap! I'll have to move back in with my mother!"

None of what she said made sense to him, but she was American and most of it likely had naught to do with him and could be dismissed out of hand. But her insistence upon the year was beginning to annoy him. He was well educated. She need not speak to him as if he knew not how to read or write—or tell the date.

He stomped out of the room and down the hall to his study and tried not to be so terribly pleased when she followed him like a curious puppy. He sat upon his chair behind the desk only to have her come 'round behind him and peer over his shoulder. His hands shuffled through papers with little purpose while he was so very distracted by her proximity. It had been a long time since he'd had such close contact with a female. Other than the women at court slithering their hands around his arms, he'd had little chance to put his hands on a woman, let alone lift her into his embrace and feel her weight. And now, there she was, leaning against his chair, brushing his shoulder.

He wondered where her other hand was in relation to the back of his neck, then shivered. He was fair to certain she was touching a strand of his hair. It took a deep breath to remember what he was about. Grasping a stack of posts from the corner of the desk, he lifted them within her reach. There would be plenty there to prove the year.

She took them and walked around the desk, taking a seat opposite him. The fact she was not blushing, meant he'd likely imagined her fingers on his hair. He ignored his disappointment. She untied the first missive and read quickly. Then read the next. Her expression told him nothing.

"These are very nice," she said. "They look a little too new to be genuine antiques, but the lettering is beautiful."

"*Antiques?* Of course they're nay antiques. Ye hold me correspondence from the past month."

She looked again and grinned. "Mm hmn. Sure. Maybe you're one of those eccentrics who got a little too into character during a local re-enactment or something. I bet the tourists even tip you. But I'm not buying it." She tied the letters back into a bundle and replaced it on the desk.

"I assure ye, I doona intend to sell ye anything. Perhaps we should let the date on the wet missive decide which of us is the true...*eccentric.*"

"Fine. But there should be a punishment for the loser."

"Fine." A shiver of excitement slipped up his spine. He had never sparred verbally with a woman since his grandmother had passed on. "Choose yer punishment."

"I'd rather choose yours, thanks." She considered only moment. "I think I'll have a foot rub. And no kicking me out until I have somewhere to go and a way to get there."

"Ye wish me to rub yer..." He couldn't say it.

"My feet. Yes. It might help me appreciate that I just about lost my toes tonight."

He swallowed. "Ye intend this to be a punishment?" When had his mouth gone so dry?

"Yes. Now choose mine."

Oh, but the lass had much to learn about punishment and rewards. If she were daft, it was not his place to teach her anything at all. But if she proved to be of sound mind...Well, then, he'd like to teach her just a thing or two. At the very least, he should teach her not to go about inviting men to touch her feet.

"Well, Mr. McKinnon? What will my punishment be if it's really 1806? Although, if it's really 1806, I think that would be punishment enough."

He ignored the jibe. "If I win, it will mean ye are completely mad. I canna punish a mad woman."

"Oh yeah? If I win, that means *you* belong in a loony bin, but I'm not too proud to take advantage of you before the guys show up with their little white truck. I'll have my foot rub before they drag you away."

The image of Brianna Colby being dragged away to an asylum made him quite uncomfortable. Of course he'd never be the one to expose her, but one of them was in error, and it was she.

"Fine. I'll collect a reward when the letter is read."

"Great. What is it? Not that you'll be getting it, but we should at least pretend you have a chance."

"A kiss then." He would swear to The Almighty Himself that he'd intended to say no such thing. But he had to admit, whatever else he might have intended to say, he could not recall.

For a moment, they sat in silence. He wondered whether or not she'd heard his declaration or if perhaps he'd merely heard the words in his head. Perhaps she was waiting—

"A kiss? From me?" Her face was utterly pink.

His breath quickened against his control, but he would not take it back. In truth, it was the only thing he truly desired at the moment.

He nodded once.

"Okay," she said, her voice a bit smaller than before. "When do we open the letter?"

Was she anxious to be kissed, or to be touched? Either way, he was flattered in a way much different than the empty flattery of those women in Edinburg. And he had so little to anticipate, he thought dragging it out a bit might prove entertaining.

"First thing on the morrow," he said, and he'd be damned if she didn't look a mite disappointed. He pretended not to notice. "Let us return to the parlor. We all sleep there tonight. I'd not planned to keep more than one room warm, and I dare not leave the cherub alone. When I found her skin cold to the touch..." He shook his head, unable to finish.

"I know. Popsicle. That was so weird. I can't believe she isn't sick."

He could not help but ask, "Ye said that word before. What does it mean, *popsicle*?"

"You know. Frozen on a stick?" Then she laughed and stood. "Ah, you're still playing the game. I get it. But come morning, you're going to be rubbing my feet."

"Come morning, I'll be collecting that kiss, Brianna Colby." He let her move ahead of him. Then, under his breath, he muttered, "And ye'll be begging for another."

Considering the manner in which her spine straightened, he was sure she'd heard it. The fact she did not protest gave him hope—when of course there was nothing to hope for.

CHAPTER SEVEN

Heathcliff slept like the dead—for nearly four hours—and when he woke, he felt as if it was Christmas morn and not Christmas Eve. He was about to collect a kiss. What else might make a man rise so happily with the sun, even if that sun was obstructed from view by a belligerent storm?

With his feet still on the floor, he reclined on the chaise with a small lass to one side and a woman to the other. Neither of them had stirred as yet, so he took just a moment to relish the illusion of a wee family comfortably mashed together.

The cherub turned her head and opened her amazing blue eyes. Blue like a July sky, happy as only a child could be. As if she hadn't a care in the world. As if there was no one she missed. As if she'd been his all her life. And in that moment, his heart broke for wishing it had been true.

Miss Colby stirred from his side and leaned away from him, slipping back to sleep, or possibly never having awakened at all.

Heathcliff looked at the damaged envelope. Had the wee lass overheard their conversation? Was she also anxious to see what the missive contained?

He already knew what date he'd find within, but he was curious to know what other clarity the message might bestow. The illusion of a proper family would not lift from his mind, but he could not begin to reach for such a dream—with a different woman, of course—until all his questions were answered.

Who was this coachman? Why had he delivered Brianna Colby to his door? How had he disappeared so quickly? Was there a spy within his household, helping the man to hide so completely from view? And how would the woman react when she could no longer insist the year was over 200 years in the future? Would she cease her teasing? Had she somehow convinced herself that it was true? For of a certainty, she would never be able to convince him.

The wee lass sat up, freeing him to reach for the envelope. He turned it over and reached for the opening, but his hand stilled. Perhaps there were answers within that he would not wish to know.

Nonsense.

He wanted only truth. He could rest only when he knew the whole of it. Perhaps the coachman had written to him, explaining from whence the woman hailed, to whence she must be returned. Perhaps she had escaped?

He shook the thought from his head. No wisdom in borrowing trouble. He would deal with whatever truths he could find. What other choice had he?

He opened the envelope and slid out the letter.

First of all, the letter had no date. Odd, that, since it was customary to note the date on messages of any sort. Secondly, it proved his first suspicions had been correct after all. He should have closed his door and allowed Miss Brianna Colby to become a popsicle, whatever that proved to be.

He could no longer stand to sit so near her, so he jumped to his feet and began pacing. One glance at the cherub's smile proved his abrupt change of mood had no effect on her. Would that he could keep it that way.

"There's a good lass. Do you remember the room in which ye played yesterday? The nursery? With the toys?"

She nodded, her eyes lighting with interest.

"Do ye suppose ye could find that room?"

She nodded and jumped to her feet.

"And will ye return to me if the room is cold? It has the morning sun, but promise me ye'll return straight away if you find it cold."

She nodded again, then put her fingers to her mouth and moved them away quickly, as if she'd blown him a kiss, but missed her lips.

"That means thank you." The woman's voice intruded over his shoulder.

He waited for the child to leave, then turned to face his enemy—for he must see her as the enemy now. Nothing more. Nothing softer, for pity's sake.

"This," she made the same motion the wee lass had made, "means thank you. It also means you're welcome."

Of course he'd stow the knowledge away and try it with the wee one later, but not until after Brianna Colby was hell and gone from his doorstep.

She noticed the letter in his hand, then looked at the envelope still sitting on the table before the fire.

"You opened it without me? It says 2012, doesn't it? You don't look too happy about it, so you must have lost. But since my feet are feeling just fine this morning, I'd like to change your punishment."

"I'm not surprised in the least. Disappointed, of course, but nay surprised." He was surprised, however, that she was not more nervous about what the letter might contain.

Her brow raised. "Are you okay? It wasn't that big of a deal, you know. Just a joke. You didn't really think it was 1806 did you?"

"I would hear what ye have in mind for my punishment." He was boiling with rage inside and hoped she would say something incriminating so he could release his frustration into the room.

"I think you should have to buy a computer and a cell phone. Maybe a satellite phone, considering the remote location." She smiled, pleased with herself.

"And I suppose I should send ye on this purchasing trip on me behalf? Perhaps send you with enough money to purchase aught else ye deem necessary for me home?"

She frowned and stood. "What's wrong? Has something happened? You're back to being an... Back to not being nice."

He held up the letter. Perhaps she was unaware her accomplice was going to write her. And if that was so, he would relish the look on her face when she realized she'd been exposed. He wanted to draw it out, make her squirm, make her pay for the blow he'd suffered when he'd read the letter.

"I will give ye one chance, Brianna Colby. One chance to confess all. I am not above forgiveness when given honesty."

He took a step toward her. She took a step away. It was a heady dance, this stalking. And he was in no hurry for it to end.

"Confess? Me?" She edged around the chaise. He kept advancing. "Just what do you think I need to confess to?"

"That is the point of the confession, lass. *Ye* tell *me*."

The silly woman eventually backed herself into a corner, but still he followed.

"Why did you send the girl away?" She'd whispered the question. The sound of it did disturbing things to him, as did the knowledge that they were completely alone.

The enemy, he thought. *Remember, she is the enemy*.

But still, his heart tripped. Tripped again. A deep breath in, then out. It made little difference. He could not hold another thought in his head. His only purpose now, was to kiss her.

And what harm would a kiss cause?

He could think of nothing.

"Fine. I confess," she whispered. "I'd rather have a kiss for my reward. Okay? Are you happy now?"

Was he happy? He was in hell. And her speaking aloud of the kiss he was determined to take? It should sober him. He should turn and put space between them. He should walk about in the snow outside, perhaps with his feet bare, to remember his purpose. And still, he advanced.

She hid her shaking hands behind her back and waited. When the toes of his stockinged feet mingled with hers, he leaned down, breathing her in. He measured the moment, tucking each rise of her chest into his memory, to relive later.

How sad, that it would all be relegated to memory.

With his mouth an inch from hers, he murmured, "There was no date on the letter lass. I win. I claim my prize."

Their lips brushed past, then returned, hers pressing forward as much as his. But he wanted to ensure she would remember it, this one and only kiss between them. He teased, sipped the taste of her, his lips a whisper against her own, then he pressed in again, renewing the heat they'd begun with, stealing her breath away.

Then he stepped back and did the only thing that would ensure it would never happen again.

He wiped the back of his hand across his mouth.

She frowned.

He smiled. "I'll just read this to ye, shall I?"

She took a step to her right, but he cut her off, herding her back into her corner. Then he held her there, with the fingers of one hand pushing gently but firmly against her collar bones. He ignored the heat emanating from her body, slipping easily through the thin layer of her shirt, and read.

"Dearest Brianna,

McKinnon promised all he had, so that is just what we shall take from him. Play yer part well. I shall come to collect it all, including the child, at Midnight on New Year's Eve.

"It was signed, *Ever Your Coachman*." Heathcliff turned his attention back on his prey and leaned forward. "Now, ye will tell me who is this coachman and what the pair of ye have planned. Then ye will help me catch this villain and perhaps not hang for yer part in it!"

"My part in it? Are you freaking kidding me?" She tried to push him away and when she could not, she stretched up on her toes until her nose was nigh to his chin. "I don't have anything to do with this guy. He has to be messing with you. And I can't believe he's still messing with me!"

Heathcliff held his ground. If he but let all the breath escape his lungs, his lips would rest upon hers. So close. So easy. So ridiculous.

He straightened and retreated half a step. She rocked back to her heels. Nearly two feet separated their lips, then. Relief would have been appropriate, not loss.

"The missive is clear enough," he said quietly. "Besides, last eve, when ye told me how ye teach mute children, I confessed how I promised *all I have* in exchange for someone like ye. No other heard that promise but Brianna Colby and a child that canna speak. Unless this coachman was sent by Satan himself, he heard the tale from yer own lips."

CHAPTER EIGHT

Bree refused to panic.

Even when Laird Gorgeous swung a blanket under his arm, snatched up her re-packed suitcase, and dragged her along behind him, up the lovely staircase she had no chance to admire. Even when he led her back to the bedroom where she'd first seen the little girl. Even when he tossed the blanket on the bed and stalked toward her.

She could honestly admit it was *not* panic that made her heart thump like a hammer in her chest—cause she was pretty sure it was just the adrenaline leftovers from that kiss he'd given her. Since she was still floating in a bit of pink haze, she had a hard time believing the murderous look in his eyes. But there was something else in those dark eyes she did believe.

Pain.

He stepped up to her, close enough to kiss her, then glared down instead.

"Ye will stay here until I can bear the sight o' ye again. The midday sun will warm the room."

"Why do you want to keep me around if you don't believe me?" She tried not to stare at his lips while she spoke. "Why don't you just let me leave? I'll find a way back to civilization on my own. I promise I have nothing to do with this. Whatever you have going on with that old man, you can work it out without me around."

He looked at her for the longest time. Just breathing. She had no clue what he was thinking.

"You will stay—as my guest—until the blackheart returns. I'll not give ye leave to lurk about the place waiting for a chance to take the child, or anything else, from me home."

She really wished he wanted to keep her around for romantic reasons, but as the pink fog cleared, it was obvious their kiss hadn't affected them both the same.

"That's kidnapping," she pointed out. Even in Scotland, the chance of breaking the law had to make him reconsider. He couldn't seriously be planning on holding her prisoner until New Year's Eve. So maybe this was just his knee jerk reaction. You can't fight knee jerk reactions. So maybe he'd change his mind when he cooled down a bit.

And *midnight*? Couldn't the old man have been a little more original? It was right out of a Cinderella story—only the prince was going to be disappointed when instead of a glass slipper left behind, he'd get a clunky red rainboot.

"I prefer to think of it as Scottish Hospitality—the traditional kind."

Great. It was obviously going to take him a while to calm down and see reason. She'd just have to grin and bear it for a while.

Speaking of baring it...

"What about a bathroom?" She needed one.

"Ye'll have no need for bathing for a good while." He turned toward the door.

"I don't want a bath. I need a...a water closet."

He paused. If he said he didn't know what a water closet was, she was going to lose her Colby Calm, and then she'd end up wetting her pants.

"There is a chamber pot below the bed."

A chamber pot? Was he out of his mind?

"And food?"

"Ye'll not starve, but ye will stay put. Unless of course ye can fly as ye claim to have the power to do. Oh, but I forget," he sneered. "The coachman has yer valuable charms that allow ye to do so." He looked back at her when he pulled the door open. The pain was still there.

And then he was gone.

She strode to the door and gave it a good banging. "I was with you the whole time!"

And damn it if she didn't end up using the stupid chamber pot. The whole time she was squatting over it, she expected the bastard to walk in on her. She nearly pulled muscles in her ears listening for his breathing on the other side of the door.

As it turned out, she didn't need the sun to warm the room since she worked up quite a sweat stomping around. When she got tired of veering around the bed, she pulled it into the middle of the room so she'd have a nice uninterrupted path. At the end of an hour, she wondered if she really was going crazy for the simple fact she'd enjoyed the exercise.

She never enjoyed exercise!

She was supposed to fly home on the twenty-ninth. And she had to come up with some ID before she could do that. If she had to use her rent money for a later flight, she'd have to move back in with her parents and that was *not* going to happen.

She had to get out of there. Just as soon as the storm was over. And no matter what, she couldn't let him kiss her again. No trust, no kiss. That was her new policy.

Boredom led to dozing off, but it more than made up for the lack of sleep the night before. She woke to the sound of footsteps coming down the hall and jumped to her feet.

Then she sat again, worried about looking guilty. But that just pissed her off. She wasn't guilty here. The old man was using her to play some kind of sick joke!

McKinnon opened the door wide, then looked for her before he walked in. He carried a tray to the nightstand and set it down.

"Afraid I might jump you?" she asked and rolled her eyes. "I guess you don't have to worry about that if you're going to starve me to death."

He snorted. "'Tis not yet noon, Miss Colby. Have ye turned to bone already?"

Not yet noon? She would never last. No matter how long he planned to keep her there, she would never last. She would just have to harass him into letting her leave.

"I can't believe you'd lock me up on Christmas Eve," she said dejectedly. "Christmas Eve!"

He raised an eyebrow. "Is it now? Well, then, ye'll have to forgive me. I'm so terrible at readin' calendars, and dates. I have an especially difficult time with the year, or so I've been told. Are ye certain it's Christmas Eve? Not All Hallows Eve?"

Great. He had his emotions back under control. She could tell because his brogue was a lot more tame. The last time he'd been in the room, he'd been harder to understand.

"Oh, I'm positive it's Christmas Eve. And you'd better start acting like it."

He barked with laughter. "Or what, Miss Colby? I fail to see anything ye might have with which to threaten me, while I on the other hand can threaten ye with a wee noose if ye try to steal m' wee bairn, or aught else from m' home."

"I meant that you'd better start acting like it's Christmas Eve if you don't want to break that child's heart."

He lowered his chin, giving the same impression as a bull about to charge. There was the button to push. It might even turn out to be the button that got her out of this nightmare.

"What do ye mean?" he asked quietly. "What is this risk to the cherub's heart?"

She took a moment to imagine what it would be like to have a man like him worrying about her own heart. Then she stopped herself and shook her head before she ended up sighing like a teenager.

"I mean, if you don't do something to make Christmas nice for her, she'll always remember how you let her down. She won't ever be able to get her hopes up for Christmas again."

He frowned like he didn't understand English.

"Her hopes? What might she be hoping for?"

Like a rat in a trap! Hah!

"Presents, Sherlock. Christmas Presents. A Christmas tree? Decorations? Please tell me you've got something for her to open in the morning."

"Presents? Ye mean *gifts*?" He looked horrified.

The guy really was terrified of dropping the whole 'daddy' ball wasn't he? Well, it served him right if he hadn't planned to do something special for the girl for Christmas, even if he'd only been a daddy for a day.

"Know ye what the child might be hoping for?" He tried to sound demanding, like he could bully her into helping him, but it was that intense brogue that proved how rattled he was.

She tried not to smile. "Well, hmn. I don't know. I suppose if I could use sign language, and if she understood sign language, I could ask her. But not in here. I won't help you so long as you keep me in here."

He took a step toward the door and held out an arm to let her go ahead of him. She plopped her butt back down on the bed. He closed his eyes. When his lips moved, she guessed he was praying for patience. It was kind of heady, this ability to control someone else's emotions. No wonder David kept her around for so long, for someone to toy with.

Bree promised herself, then and there, that unless her safety or her freedom was at stake, she would only use her new super powers for good. She tried really hard not to giggle as she hopped to her feet and hurried out the door.

* * *

They found the girl dancing around in a room that looked like an ancient nursery. She was wearing the little grey dress and black lace-up boots McKinnon had taken from the bedroom. Her clothes looked as much like a costume as her daddy's and Bree realized it must be the way people dressed in the Highlands. With how cold it was, maybe they had to pay more attention to warmth than style. Still, the child would have looked less like an urchin if McKinnon added a little pink to her wardrobe. There was a little black dress still hanging on a hook in the bedroom and Bree was afraid that was all the kid had.

All the toys looked hand made. There were three little beds and a cradle, all hand-carved and without mattresses. It was the kind of place you'd expect to be haunted by the ghosts of children. The thought made Bree shiver.

The girl didn't seem to notice she was no longer alone, so Bree opened her mouth to call out her name. Then she realized she didn't know it.

"McKinnon, what is the girl's name?"

He glanced at the floor, then looked away. "I call her Cherub."

"Surely that's not her real name."

"I was never given her name. The nurse disappeared before I could ask. Not unlike your coachman." He was daring her to disbelieve him, she guessed.

Bree whistled. The girl turned to her immediately, those little blue eyes wide with wonder. Had she never heard a whistle before?

Each interaction with the child had Bree more and more convinced that her inability to speak was more of an emotional issue than a physical one, especially considering the child was able to hear normally. And if Bree wasn't able to help the child before she escaped the McKinnon Loony Bin, she'd make sure Pseudo Daddy knew how to get the kid the help she would need.

And some pink outfits.

"Hey, pumpkin!" Bree gave her a big smile.

McKinnon grunted. She ignored him.

"I think it is time you told me your name," she said, both with her voice and her hands. Although the girl could hear, she would be more at ease, signing, if she weren't the only one doing it.

The girl shrugged her shoulders and started dancing again.

Bree caught her shoulder and shook her head. Then signed and spoke again, showing her the signs that went along with the words. "My name is Bree." She signed the letters slowly. The girl copied her.

"Very good! You're so clever! You learn so quickly." Again she added the signs to what she said. "Your...name...is..." She left the words hanging, hoping the girl would finish.

Then little Miss Cherub signed, *I have no name*. She gave a little shrug then went back to dancing.

McKinnon cleared his throat. She wasn't going to make him beg, but it took a minute for the surprise to wear off before she could face him. It was just so sad! *If* the girl was telling the truth. But she'd seen no reason to think the kid was playing them.

"Well?"

Bree said quietly, "She says she has no name."

He winced. Poor guy. He'd already said the kid couldn't be his, so he shouldn't be taking on the blame if the child hadn't been properly cared for. Well, at least enough to have some sense of identity. Someone must have cared enough to have her taught how to sign. That was kind of a big deal. And she had to admit, the girl hadn't seemed particularly sad about anything else, just not having a name. And she didn't look too sad about that, really.

"You're just going to have to give her a name, that's all. And it can't be Cherub or Pumpkin, or something silly. She's going to want a real name."

The girl twirled around and caught Bree's hands, then pulled her into a music-less dance. Bree didn't want to mess with whatever tune was playing in the girl's head, so she picked up the rhythm and danced along silently.

McKinnon watched. At first, he watched the child dancing with a mixture of longing and pity on his face. But then he started to frown. Bree could feel the storm clouds gathering in his brain and knew he was going to open his mouth and become that jackass again.

She shook her head at him while she spun past.

"What is the matter with you now?"

"Ye have yet to ask her what she hopes to find in a Christmas gift."

Bree stopped dancing and got the girl's attention.

"Do you know what tomorrow is?" she asked and signed.

The girl nodded, then made the sign for Christmas. At least it could have been interpreted as Christmas.

"And what do you hope you get for Christmas, young lady?"

The child didn't even hesitate. She made the sign for the moon and pointed at the window.

Great. Something McKinnon couldn't get her. He wasn't going to be happy.

"And what did she say?" he asked gruffly. She started to think he had read the sign just fine, but she said it anyway.

"She says she's expecting the moon."

Only after the words left her mouth did she realize how bad it sounded, like the kid thought she was going to get the world laid at her feet—like she might be expecting to come into a lot of money.

McKinnon knelt on one knee and held out a hand. The child hurried to take it.

"Tell me, Cherub," he said gently. "Have ye heard Miss Colby and I speak of a coachman?"

The child nodded.

"And do ye ken this coachman? Have ye ever met him yerself?"

The kid grinned, then nodded again.

Five minutes later, Bree and Miss Cherub were munching down Bree's lunch—the lunch left back in her little prison, the prison the two of them were apparently going to share.

CHAPTER NINE

Heathcliff was aware that the horrible day he'd lived through on the twenty third of December paled in horror to the twenty-fourth. But that did not mean he couldn't fight back. Unfortunately, he didn't know whom he needed to fight.

Why did he not see it before?

Their hair was so similar in shade. They were both able to speak with their hands. Of course he knew there was a school in Paris for deaf people, teaching new ways to communicate. Perhaps it was their ability to do so silently that convinced the coachman the lasses made a fine pair of accomplices. The woman could easily pass a message to the man through the very window, as could the child.

Perhaps they'd been compelled to help him.

Of course his heart was grasping for any reason that might redeem the two blondes from villainy. The cruelest crime they'd committed, however, was to give him the weakest thread of hope that the child might remain in his keeping, only to take away that hope. Like sending a boat for a drowning sailor—a boat with a gaping hole.

From the start he'd known, somehow, that the child would be taken from him. It was simply too miraculous to be true. He'd feared it from the moment she'd been left with him.

And she'd been as good as taken from him already.

At the thought, pain arced through his chest like a mean bit of lightning. It was likely only a taste of the pain that would have come if he'd spent another week playing father only to find she was part of the conspiracy.

Yes. It was a lucky thing he'd caught on right away.

To be truly helpful, his Muir blood should have warned him to leave town days ago, instead of warning him, too late, that wickedness approached. By then, the wicked had already been inching their way toward his heart.

But there was more wickedness afoot, and he was going to discover it.

With the only key to the room tucked into his pocket, he was free to turn his castle upside down if necessary to find those who would aid the little thieves. If his suspicions proved true, the lass was not his responsibility. But even so, it was reassuring to know that she was looked after. Surely, as the child's mother, or older sister at least, the woman could keep her safe, warm, fed... Dear lord, but the fatherly concerns were going to take a fine time leaving him.

If the woman had never come along, he'd be the happiest adoptive father alive and none would be able to take the lass from him without a fight to the death. But he would entertain not another moment of hope if it might break his heart in the end. He'd had enough.

For fear of flushing any culprits outside and away, he started out of doors and worked inward, hoping to corner the guilty inside the castle. He'd barred the front door from the outside. Thanks to the heavy snow, it took little enough effort to do so. A sturdy board shored up the ice already forming against the thick wood. As most castle doors did, it opened outward, but not this day.

The weight of the barbican gate was enough to close out any stealthy carriage deliveries, or collections—of any one or any thing.

The stables held no surprises. No strange mounts huddled there against the still raging storm. No fresh footprints in the snow. All his animals had long since been moved down into the glen for the winter. The only things left in his care for the twelve days of Christmas were his own mount, Macbeth, and the goose he was to roast for his Christmas supper. The pair had been sheltered inside the stone barn together and it was likely the harassment from the goose that kept Macbeth moving and therefore, warm. It also meant that in making itself useful, the goose had won another day of life.

"The pair of you should be grateful for each other. Ye'll both still be alive for Christmas."

Heathcliff closed up the barn and checked the rest of the out buildings but found not a sign of disturbance. Few of the structures were still in use, but they'd been built too well to see torn down. By the time the nineteenth century arrived, his family castle was no longer a bustling town unto itself; the villagers had gradually distanced themselves from the home of the Muir Witch in spite of it also being home to their laird. After his grandmother died, activity increased in and out of the castle, but none lived too near.

Managing his tenants and investments kept him busy enough during the day. When a man has no family to distract him, he has time to improve both his own lot and that of his people. Truth be told, if he did nothing but sit on his arse and grow fat, his wealth would continue to grow. And if being the grandson of a Muir Witch was his first problem, his money was his second. It was easy to suspect anyone who showed up on his doorstep.

But a child? Even a child he'd come to care for? Had hoped to make his own?

What the devil had become of him?

Heathclilff stopped in his tracks, struck immobile by his thoughts. Was it the fresh air that helped him to think more clearly?

He often thought of his home as a large empty box made of stone. No wife and children waiting inside for him. But that day, as he stood knee-deep in snow, ignoring the buffeting of the wind as it tried to push him out of his boots, there *was* a woman and child waiting inside.

Of course the letter made it clear the woman, to whom he was unusually attracted, was conspiring against him and should not be trusted. But the cherub? What had possessed him to ask the child if she knew the coachman? Doesn't every child know a coachman? What if she hadn't understood that he was asking about a specific man?

What a coward he was! He'd been given a miracle and for fear of a bit of bruising to his heart, he'd doubted it.

But perhaps the damage could be undone.

"The pair of ye should be grateful for each other." It was if the wind blew his own words back to him. And yet, the sound still hummed in his ears. It hadn't been a memory at all. The words had been murmured! And not by him!

He whipped around, expecting to find the coachman at his back.

From the drift against the barn wall, snow blew across his footprints and splattered against the old tanner's cottage, like a massive ghost moving from one grave to the next.

"Show yerself!" His voice boomed loud and clear, chasing away the murmur, shaking the roof of the stable just behind him.

He heard a roar but had no time to turn before he felt a terrible weight crash into his back, force his breath from him, and send him into oblivion.

* * *

After extensive experimentation, Bree proved that rubbing two sticks together was not the key to starting a fire. It helped warm her up, but she wasn't sure it if was due to exercise or anger, just like before.

How could that man just let them freeze?

Sitting cross legged on the floor in front of the hearth, she pulled the quilts off the little girl and draped them over her own shoulders, then opened her arms so the kid could crawl onto her lap.

"We're just going to have to keep cuddling until he comes," she said.

The kid rolled her eyes and grinned, her shaking shoulders the only indication she was laughing—or would have been laughing if she had a voice. Then she bent and collected the little box of odds and ends Bree hadn't been able to make odds and ends out of.

"I don't think you should be playing with that," Bree said, but didn't take the stuff away from her. What was the worst that could happen? She'd start a fire?

And damned if she didn't!

Sparks shot out from between the rock and the metal thingee, landed on the fluffy stuff and caught fire! A minute later, actual pieces of wood were lighting up.

"So sue me," she said. "I'm a city girl. My idea of girl's camp was going to a hotel to swim and have a sleepover."

It was getting late in the afternoon, but the shadows that had been falling were chased away by their happy little fire. The little girl sat down on Bree's lap, but jumped back to her feet in surprise when Bree's stomach growled.

Bree laughed. "I guess I'm hungry. Are you getting hungry?"

The girl shrugged and climbed into the chair. The room was warming enough so they no longer needed to sit so close to the flames. Bree got up and draped a blanket around the kid so her back wouldn't get cold, then she went to the lunch tray to see if there was anything left that the girl might eat. And maybe if Laird Gorgeous-but-Mean heard them moving around, it might remind him there was someone in the castle besides himself.

She bent over the tray and found just what she'd expected. Nothing. They'd been pretty hungry at lunchtime too.

Something large crashed downstairs.

Bree stepped to the door and pressed her ear against it.

She could hear him moving around down there, but the door was thick and she couldn't tell much, only that someone was making noises. Clumsy noises.

Is he drunk?

Man, if they'd been freezing their butts off because he'd been drinking and forgot about them, she was going straight to the police as soon as she got out of there. No way would he get custody of a child he'd nearly frozen to death not once, but twice!

She heard stomping on the stairs. But he only took a few steps, then stopped. Then started again. Her anger bubbled hotter every time he stopped. Was he messing with them?

The whole point of coming to Scotland was to get a better grasp on her life. To take control again, to find herself again. But since she'd stepped off the train in Burnshire, she'd lost control completely.

She'd lost the tour she'd been so excited about.

She'd lost control of her senses and set out in a snowstorm, in an unsafe car that she'd also lost control of.

She'd been used as a pawn in the game of some insane old man so the loveliest man she'd ever met in her life thought the smart thing to do would be to lock her up.

Now the only thing she could control was a freaking chamber pot.

Aaand...

She couldn't even pretend this bedroom was her personal safe space because the danger of freezing to death made it anything but safe!

If the lovely idiot could somehow make his way to the top of the stairs and come open her door, she was going to bloody take control if it killed her.

Bree's heart jumped when he finally reached the hall. It sounded like he was sliding along the wall, which gave her hope because if he was that drunk, he'd be a lot easier to overpower.

He slammed against the door. She jumped back. It was so hard to picture him that wasted, she suddenly wondered if their visitor wasn't McKinnon at all!

Heavy breathing pushed through and around the edge of the door.

She tried not to freak out; after all, she had a little girl to worry about too. She hurried over to the chair, scooped up the child, wrapped the blanket tighter and hurried to the bed.

"We're going to play a trick on Laird McKinnon," she whispered. "You're going to hide under the bed. Okay? Don't be scared. He's going to think it's funny."

She waited for the girl to nod before she laid her under the edge of the bed and gently pushed her back as far as she could. She didn't have to remind her to be quiet. Then she went back to the door and forced herself to move close, to listen again.

"Brianna," a man whispered. "Brianna. Open the door."

If it was McKinnon, he would know it was locked from the outside.

"Brianna. Please."

She heard something metal hit the hall floor. Then a stomp. A key flew under the door and hit her foot. She picked it up, then listened again. She wasn't going to open the door to anyone but McKinnon, even if he'd given her a key.

"Brianna." The voice was a bit stronger this time. "Cherub! Open the door."

Only McKinnon would call the child Cherub!

Bree inserted the key and turned the lock. When she lifted the latch, the door pushed open with McKinnon's weight behind it. She managed to stay on her feet, then caught him as he fell forward. Her strength was no match for someone twice her size and she went down. He fell on top of her with a grunt.

"McKinnon. Are you drunk?" She couldn't smell alchohol.

"F..f...frozen," he stammered. "Why...why...why is my d...daughter beneath th..the bed?"

Bree looked up to find the little girl grinning at them with the orange firelight lighting her face like the sun. She hadn't moved, she was still wrapped up like a quilted burrito.

"Because I didn't think the man staggering against the door would be you." Bree pushed on his right shoulder and he stiffly rolled off her, with a lot of help. When she was on her feet she realized just how stiff he was. "Were you trying to find out just what it felt like to be a popsicle?"

She moved to the door and shut it, to keep the heat in the room, and while her back was turned, she casually dropped the key into her bra, then she tossed plenty of wood on the fire.

"N...not by choice. I was b...b...buried in the s...snow. A...avalanche. S...stables. W...what are ye doing?"

He actually looked scared as she started to peel off his layers of coats.

"The heat can't get to you through all your clothes." She pulled a stiff arm straight and tugged off a sleeve. "Just be glad you're not too wet."

"I humbly beg yer pardon," he said.

"For what?"

"If th...this is how ye felt when ye were left on me doorstep last eve."

Wow. It was nice to have him believe her about something, even if it was just about how cold she'd been.

"I forgive you. Now, let me have your pants."

CHAPTER TEN

Heathcliff was relieved each and every time Brianna returned to the bedchamber. She'd gone to the kitchens for water and hauled it up the stairs. She'd heated the water, made him soak his hands in it, then gone to fetch them all some supper. She'd also gone in search of wood and returned with much more than she should have attempted to carry, wee lass that she was.

He'd balked at nothing except for her request that he relinquish his trousers. It was bad enough manners to bask in the heat of the fire without a shirt, in the presence of females, but after he'd noted her reaction to his physique, he'd swallowed his pride. 'Twas a fact her attention was drawn to his chest whenever it seemed there was nothing else in the room for her to examine.

It served her rightly, of course. He'd been fighting a similar battle with his own eyes since she'd first peeled off her extra clothing, and if he were honest, before then as well. There was something about her face his eyes found soothing.

And something about her lips...

She had donned her strange gray trousers and the gray knitted sweater, so at least his attention was able to settle on something besides her bare calves. There was a bit of an ankle showing now and again due to the shortness of her stockings, however. They served as slippers, he supposed, but with all her scurrying about on the dusty floor, they were quickly turning gray as well.

The cherub had fallen asleep soon after eating, as had he. But he woke to find that the woman had still not abandoned them. As he sat in the chair fairly roasting before the freshly stoked fire, she bent over him to feel his forehead. She'd removed her sweater. Perhaps the heat was getting uncomfortable for her as well.

"You feel okay to me." Her fingers fell to his chest just before she straightened. Even in the firelight, her blush was evident. His chest burned where her fingers had been.

"Oh? Perhaps ye'd care to examine me fingers?" He held them out for inspection.

She grasped his hands in hers and her brows flew high. She pulled him forward, toward the fire, then she began rubbing both hands and fingers as if his very life depended on it. When his upper limbs had been duly massaged, she demonstrated how he should wiggle them in front of the flames. As if he didn't know how to warm himself.

"You're going to be lucky not to have frostbite, Mr. McKinnon. Seriously."

Though he appreciated being fussed over, he did not care to be addressed as Mr. McKinnon. Especially after she'd been rubbing his fingers with such familiarity only a moment before.

"Laird," he said. "Laird McKinnon. Or ye may call me Heathcliff. One or the other, if ye please.

She snorted. "Well, I'm not about to call you Laird."

Inwardly, he smiled. He hadn't suspected she would do so either. And so she would have no choice but to call him by his given name. He'd liked the sound of it on her tongue before. And even though she still could not be trusted, she had just fussed him back from a frozen grave. He owed her something for that at least.

"You called her your daughter," she said while she stepped to the side of the hearth and settled herself against the wall, away from the immediate heat of the flames. "When you first came in, you called her your daughter again. Does that mean you're done suspecting her?"

"Aye." He scooted his chair back, but when she gave him a frown, he extended his fingers and wiggled them as he'd been shown.

She laughed. The sound of it did strange things inside his chest. Just like the lightning he'd felt before, but not painful.

"When you asked her if she knew the coachman, she probably just nodded to try and make you happy."

"That was my conclusion as well."

"Good," she said, but she'd stopped smiling. "Now that that's out of the way, I think we should have a serious talk."

"Serious?"

"Serious means you're not going to like it."

"I see. Very well. What would ye care to discuss?" He crossed his arms and felt quite powerful when her gaze locked on his chest and upper arms. He flattered himself to think the lass might just forget what she had been about to say, for it took a wee while for her to blink.

Eventually, she shook her head and looked into his eyes for a change.

"The year," she said.

He snorted. "Yer year, or mine?"

"Exactly." She sat forward and twisted her hands in her lap. "I've just been in your kitchen, Mr... Heathcliff. Now, either you're trying to keep this place looking medieval for the tourists, or you're doing it for yourself, because you like pretending you're the king of the castle, or whatever. I appreciate that your clothes are pretty authentic looking too, for the 1800's. But whatever you've got going on here, you have to admit that it's against the law—in the real world—to hold me here against my will."

"Agreed."

She'd taken a breath, no doubt prepared for an exhaustive argument, but let the air out slowly, then frowned.

"You agree? You admit that it's Christmas Eve, 2012?"

Christmas Eve!

"Lass. I beg yer pardon, but we'll have to continue this discussion on the morrow. There are some things I need to do, ye see, before I can find me bed for the night."

"Are you going to start a fire somewhere else? Or are you going to spend the night in here?"

He lifted a brow. She could not have meant the question to sound so...inviting.

"In here, with *us*," she said, looking pointedly at the lump on the bed.

"Ah, I thank ye for the lovely invitation, but no. Dinna worry over saving some wood for morning. I'll have more then." He paused at the door. "Keep each other warm."

"And who will keep you warm, Heathcliff?" It sounded more like concern than seduction, so he answered it as such.

"I'll go and make a fire now, Brianna. I promise not to end me life as a...popsicle."

Once he was out the door, his mind began to race. So much to do. So little time.

CHAPTER ELEVEN

———◦◦◦———

Bree woke cold and stiff. She'd fallen asleep spooning with the little pumpkin, and by the way that little pumpkin was dancing around the room, she clearly knew what day it was.

She only hoped Heathcliff, as she was now supposed to call him, would put forth a little bit of effort to make the day special for the girl. She glanced nervously at the closed door, then remembered that she had the key.

She checked. It was still in her bra.

Someone knocked on the door. No mystery who it was.

"Good morrow, Cherub. Brianna," he called through the door. "I've a warm fire burning in the parlor. If the pair of ye would prepare yerselves for the day and join me below stairs, ye may break your fast there as well."

His steps moved away, then came back. He knocked once.

"And Happy Christmas."

He sounded awfully cheerful. Maybe he had finally dropped the historical act and he'd be wearing jeans and a t-shirt. After imagining that for a minute, she decided Heathcliff in jeans and a t-shirt would be a great Christmas present.

She pushed away the fact that her family was going to be very disappointed when she didn't call them that day, but she'd checked the place for phones. There was no way she could make a call, so she just wouldn't waste time worrying about it.

She helped the little pumpkin into her black dress, her hose and little boots, then slipped her own cream cardigan over her little head.

"Merry Christmas," Bree told her and held out the big rhinestone flower she'd taken off her own little black dress.

The girl was so excited she could hardly stand still while Bree pinned it on the sweater, over her little heart, like a corsage. She never took her eyes off it while Bree finished dressing in the deflowered but still shiny dress. As she slipped on her gray sweater, she ignored the smell of pine smoke.

Ten minutes later, she and the pumpkin headed down the staircase. Bathing both of them with only a pitcher of icy cold water had, out of necessity, taken three minutes, tops.

The warmth from the parlor reached them before they made it all the way down the stairs, and as they neared the parlor doors, Bree was suddenly nervous.

She'd convinced herself she was wearing the dress and nylons just to prove she knew how to wear them properly, but that was a lie. She wanted to drive the guy a little crazy, like he had been driving her crazy for two days. She wanted to look so good he would have a hard time acting all suspicious and grumpy for the whole day. If she'd been able to shower and wash her hair, she might have even won another kiss. But she'd settle for civility.

The doors opened by themselves and Bree realized, in a split second, she'd been beaten at her own game.

Heathcliff McKinnon, Laird of the McKinnons, stood gripping the top of the door, dressed in complete

Scottish regalia. His green velvet coat was short-waisted and the shade matched the plaid of his kilt and the sash that went over his shoulder. She realized it was the same plaid as the drapes—green and red. She refused to look closer at the fur-covered purse that hung in front of his kilt. But she had no problem appreciating that, with one arm raised as it was, his kilt lifted on that side and showed a knee glorious enough to make Michelangelo weep.

Bree was tempted to turn around and go lock herself back in the room. This could not turn out good for her. He'd have no respect at all for a woman who followed him around the castle on all fours.

"Happy Christmas," he said and pulled the door wider.

The child ran into the room and over to a Christmas tree tipped against the wall beside the mantle. The bottom of it looked like the lord of the manor had hired a beaver to fell the thing. Bree walked closer, grateful to have something else to stare at for the moment.

It was decorated with toys from the nursery. Branches skewered the gaps beneath the bellies of the miniature rocking horses. Little toy soldiers dangled precariously by their weapons that were hooked in the pine needles. A delicate doll sat at the top with a branch shoved up her dress.

The mantle itself was covered with lit candles that competed with the brightness of the morning sun streaming through the windows. The snow had gathered in the corners of the large window panes and along with the drapes, the whole scene looked like a Christmas card—except for the fact the tree was leaning.

Bree realized the man behind her had not moved. He'd done a lot since leaving the bedroom last night. He was probably a little nervous about their reaction.

She spun on her heel and gave Heathcliff the wide smile he deserved.

"It's wonderful," she said. "And our little pumpkin thinks so too, don't you pumpkin?" She found the child standing next to her, grinning and bobbing her head. Bree looked back toward the door. "Merry Christmas, Heathcliff."

The man was frowning again, but this time at the child. "Ye didna find yer gifts?"

The little girl's eyes flew wide.

"There, by the fire." He pointed to two green velvet sacks tied shut with yellow ribbon. "The pair of them are for ye, of course. The only gift I could think of for you, Miss Brianna, is to allow ye to leave us." He looked at his hands. "Or I can allow ye free reign of the house."

The way her chest tried to cave in when he'd given her permission to leave made the decision easy. Besides, she wouldn't find much open on Christmas day, let alone find someone who might help her get her ID back.

"I'll take it," she said. "I'll stay. I've got to clear my name, right? Prove that I'm not part of that old man's joke."

"Excellent." He walked forward until he was standing next to her. Together, they watched the girl open her presents. The whole time, Bree kept glancing down to make sure his knee wasn't still showing. She had to keep reminding herself to breathe.

The biggest bundle was one of the antique dolls from the shelf in the nursery. The girl hugged it to her, but then looked at Heathcliff with a little worry on her smooth forehead.

"Yes, it is yers to keep," he said. "If ye stay or go, the doll is yers."

She closed her eyes and gave the doll a little hug before she reached for the smaller package. When it turned out to be only a little scroll, she frowned up at him again.

"Go ahead. Open it," he said.

Her little fingers slid the ribbon off the end and unrolled the paper. Then she shrugged and shook her head.

"Ye cannot yet read?" he asked. "Then I shall tell ye what it says. It is yer new name. Forevermore, this shall be yer name. You must take very fine care of it. Can ye do that?"

She nodded, probably not understanding how she would go about taking care of her name. She also looked like she was going to wet her pants if he didn't tell her what it was.

"Yer name is Angeline."

She closed her eyes and hugged the paper for ten long seconds, then she grabbed her doll and started dancing around the room.

Bree turned to the big Scot and patted the side of his chest not covered by the plaid sash. The muscle beneath the crisp cream shirt was hard as a rock.

"You did very well for your first try at Father Christmas," she said.

His dark eyelashes dropped against his cheeks as he looked at her hand. She snatched it back.

"Thank ye," he said, but she didn't know if he was thanking her for the compliment, the pat, or for getting her paws off him.

* * *

"Why is the snow on your head not melting," Brianna asked.

Heathcliff took a moment to ponder whether she was merely trying to ruin his concentration on the chess board, or whether, by some miracle there might be snow on his head. Then he remembered the goose. He reached up, felt about, then plucked a feather from his hair. He'd been afraid he'd not found them all.

"Because it is nay snow, Brianna. It is a feather." Lord how he loved the feel of her name on his tongue. "I'll have ye know it has been a very long time since I have plucked a goose. I made a bleedin' mess of it, pardon me language. I was told I should always save the downy feathers, but they're not the easiest of things to gather. Come spring, I fear we will not be sure all the snow has melted from the bailey until a determined wind comes to blow all the blasted things away."

Her eyes had widened with every word, so he'd rambled on, to see how big they might grow.

"A goose? You killed a goose? Like, a *real live goose*? I'm no vegetarian, but I can appreciate a pretty bird, you know?"

He could not help but frown. Perhaps American geese were a bit prettier than Scottish geese.

"A *live* goose? I could hardly kill a dead goose, lass."

She shrugged her pretty shoulders. "I just feel like I have blood on my hands, that's all. Did you kill this goose to feed us?"

"Now, why the bloody hell would I have killed a goose otherwise, if not to feed us? And why would the blood be on yer hands? I am the butcher today."

She frowned, considering, then nodded. He was but glad she'd given up arguing over the violence of putting food on the table. He could hardly offer them turnips for Christmas, could he?

Angeline was now holding the discarded feather between two fingers. Her wee bottom lip stuck out just a bit farther than usual, and he was not about to have the same argument with a child who could not speak.

"I am certain the bird was proud to know 'twas to be yer Christmas Goose, Angeline." Besides, he'd promised the fowl it could live until Christmas, not after. And he'd not specified how long into the day that would be. Getting the thing out of the barn was his Christmas gift to Macbeth. The horse had been harried enough and the weather had warmed a bit, even without the appearance of the sun. The beast no longer needed a goose to keep him moving and warm.

The girl looked relieved, and even happier to hear her name once again. He would have to remember to repeat it often. She grinned and blew the feather off her fingers, then raced around the room to catch and blow it all over again. Later in the day, when it came time to remove the goose from the spit, she seemed to make no connection between the meat on her plate and the feather she'd played with all the afternoon.

The blasted woman sighed over the meal a dozen times before finally taking a bite. After that, it seemed the taste of the foul was nigh fine enough to raise her appetite a bit higher than her sensitivity.

"This is wonderful," she said around a mouthful, then reached forward and ripped off a large meaty leg. For the rest of the meal, she waved it about her like Henry the Eighth while she told Angelina the most outrageous Christmas stories, including one she told in song, about a snowman who came to life one day.

The child asked, with her hands, if he might allow them to make such a snow man. He told her it would be much too cold to attempt such a thing until the following week. His answer seemed to sober Brianna who claimed to have no more Christmas stories to tell. The rest of the day was spent playing games and resting from games. He never got the chance to finish his conversation with Brianna.

"Happy Christmas, Angeline." He pressed a kiss to the pale wee forehead and tucked the child into her bed. After Brianna gave her the same treatment, the lassie dropped the doll to the floor and laid her little scroll on the pillow next to her head, then closed her eyes.

Poor mite, he thought, and turned his back, bending down to start a fire to keep Angeline warm until Brianna joined her later on the bed. It had nothing to do with the moisture gathering in his eyes.

The woman waited for him in the hallway. No doubt she did not wish to traverse the darkened stairway alone, but as he turned to precede her, she pulled on his arm to stop him. He could not ignore the warmth of her touch and when he turned back to her, he moved rather closer than he should have, for it would have been a simple thing to bend down and press his lips to hers. Simple, and natural as well.

For a moment, she said nothing.

"Are you up to granting a Christmas wish, Mister McKinnon?"

He let his frown show his displeasure at addressing him thusly.

"Fine. *Heathcliff.* Will you grant a Christmas Wish?"

"If I can."

He wondered if she would ask him for a kiss, but dared not promise to grant whatever she might ask. The lass was clever and might take advantage. At the moment, however, he hoped she would take advantage only of his proximity.

"Well, yeah. I'm starting to wonder if you can, too, but I'm going to ask anyway."

Ah, then. She was not about to ask for a kiss after all.

"If it is possible to grant your wish, I'll do so, but I'll be expecting ye to grant a wish of mine as well. Christmas and all that."

Her breath quickened. She knew exactly what he would ask. Well and good, then. If she shared her wish, she'd be agreeing to his.

"I'd like you to suspend your disbelief until New Year's Eve."

He glanced at the high ceiling while he tried to interpret her meaning. She spoke so strangely sometimes. As much as he hated to admit it—for it would likely mean the forfeit of his Christmas Kiss—he would have to concede his ignorance.

"Explain what you mean, Brianna." He so enjoyed saying her name.

"Like when you're watching a movie—suspend your disbelief. Pretend you believe me. Pretend you trust Angeline. Pretend you don't think I'm a thief. Just pretend, until we can get this straightened out. It's going to be pretty miserable around here if you can't even trust a little girl enough to let her make a freaking snowman out of Christmas snow. It's not like it's even *regular* snow. It's actual *Christmas* snow. Can't you pretend, even for a little girl, that Christmas snow could be magic?"

She was getting a bit loud, so he put a finger up to his lips, to remind her that the lass was but on the far side of the door, trying to sleep. She looked at the door and nodded her understanding, then pulled him to the head of the staircase.

"And while you're at it, you can pretend you believe that I'm just an American on vacation who got screwed over by a couple of old Scottish con artists." She dropped her chin to her chest and sighed. "That sounds so stupid! No wonder you can't believe me." She turned aside and took a step toward the chamber door. "Never mind," she said sadly.

It was his turn to stop her. Her arm was small but strong in his grasp. She barely resisted when he pulled her up against him. The sconce light barely had room to shine between their faces.

"Wait just a moment. Your Christmas Wish is to have me ignore the facts, ignore my suspicions, and pretend to believe you are as you say, and that the child has but been abandoned to my care, and the pair of ye knew nothing of each other before ye found each other here, in my home?"

She nodded and looked down again. He took one hand from her back so he could lift her chin, but kept her close. Dark blue pools shimmered just below a layer of tears that threatened to follow their fellows down the sides of her face.

"And if I can do such a simple thing as pretend for the remainder of our time together, ye'll grant my own Christmas Wish?"

She gasped and tensed beneath his touch, as if only then realizing that it was *he* who was asking for a blind promise, that perhaps he would ask for more than just a kiss from her. He should have been offended by her fear, but she was right to be wary. After all, they'd known each other but for two days, and for half that time, he'd kept her behind lock and key. She'd likely feared the worst of him long before now.

"I'll take but a kiss from ye, Brianna. I'll grant yer boon, if ye would grant mine. And I'll ask nothing more of ye, I swear it."

She nodded only slightly, but then it grew in strength as she took a deep breath and made her decision clear. Her eyes closed and her chin lifted, but he merely stood and watched, trying to instill the sight in his memory—a little vision to entertain him months from now, after he should have forgotten the shape of her face, the tilt of her brows, the dip in her bottom lip.

No, he wouldn't forget. He'd draw her, before he had the chance to forget any of it.

Her eyes opened, lifted in confusion.

He looked into them while he lowered his lips to hers, gently, firmly. Her eyes fluttered shut and he joined her in that darkness that existed only for the two of them. The kiss was perfection with a swift moving undercurrent that swept him up. He could not get close enough to her and he pulled her tight, to share his frustration.

She pushed at him and before he had his eyes open, she was out of his arms and running for the bedchamber.

"Wait!" He needed a moment to clear his head, to sort out the shadows. He could not allow her to run from him in fear, but the door was open and that shiny black dress was slipping through. "Wait! Brianna!"

As he reached her door, it closed quietly, but firmly. He felt, more than heard, the large trunk sliding across the floor. It thumped against the wood.

"Brianna," he said softly. "Forgive me. I would have never..." Well, of course he could claim no such thing. In truth, he did not know what might have happened. He'd hardly been thinking clearly. "I hope I would have controlled myself."

"Goodnight, Mr. McKinnon." Her whisper said it all.

He stepped back and straightened. "It shall not happen again, Miss Colby."

As he walked briskly to his own cold bedchamber, he hoped he was telling the truth.

CHAPTER TWELVE

It was a long night of arguing—with herself of course. She shouldn't have run. Yes, she sure as hell should have. No, I was dumb. No, I was lucky to have gotten away. For an hour, she worried what she would say to him in the morning. After she decided to say nothing at all, to let him do all the talking, she fell asleep.

She woke with a headache, but decided to ignore that too.

It would do her no good to think about what she could be doing with the rest of her vacation time—if she could get away from there. Besides, if this place was snowed in, it was likely the rest of the Highlands were too. And she'd rather be stuck in a beautifully furnished castle than exploring castle ruins in bad weather or watching Scotland stream by out the window of a bus. At least here, in McKinnon's castle, she had a much better chance of running into a painfully handsome Highlander every day. And if she ever told her friends the truth about her vacation, which wasn't likely, they would agree with her.

But why had the coachman written that note? Did he think she was someone else? Impossible. He'd asked her for her full name. He knew she wasn't his accomplice. So why write it unless he knew McKinnon would read it and it would upset him?

And would anything really happen on New Year's Eve? They had to assume so because there was a little girl involved. They had to protect her, but protect her from what? Someone who had a grudge against McKinnon?

And why didn't he go to the police?

Because he didn't have a freaking car? What kind of twilight zone had she stumbled into?

She shook her head as she left her room. She couldn't possibly be buying the whole 1806 theory. She just had to prove to McKinnon that it was time to give up the pretense. And she'd start at the top. She was a Colby, after all. No fear.

The door she believed would lead out onto the roof was blocked shut by snow, sadly. She had to settle for leaning out of windows to see the extensive bailey and outbuildings. The East tower was off-limits, Heathcliff had said, probably because it was his personal space. Since it wasn't likely she'd find enchanted things in there, like they did in movies, she didn't mind honoring his request to 'mind her own business.'

Of course he would have never said it that way.

"*Do me the honor of avoiding the East Wing,*" he'd said. Mr. Formal. Always. Just like he'd speak if he was from the 19th century, just like he'd said.

She laughed at herself. She really hadn't been drinking the Kool-Aid, had she? Besides, Heathcliff had admitted the truth on Christmas Eve. Or had he?

She continued her solo tour of Castle McKinnon that was really a quest for the tiniest proof of something twentieth century. It didn't even need to be from 2012. It just had to be something more modern than 1806.

There was nothing in the bedrooms upstairs. She checked every drawer, every shelf. Nothing. Even the wall paper looked vintage. The linens were odd, but lovely. And every bed had drapes for keeping the heat around the occupants when the fires went out during the night. That made her think of heat vents, then she couldn't find any of those either. But this was Scotland, and it was a castle; putting in a heating system would have probably cost a grundle of money. Probably more than plumbing. And electricity...

Bree found an odd pan with holes in the lid attached to a long handle. Was it a popcorn popper for over the fire? Was popcorn a modern thing? She grabbed the pan and hurried to the stairs. There was a chance she had her proof, but she would just ask, casually, what it was used for.

The warm green and red plaid dress he'd left for her kept Bree from rushing down the stairs. No wonder women in long gowns seemed more dignified—they had no choice. She had to hold onto the skirt and the pan handle with one hand and the railing with the other. If she fell down that long curve of stone steps, she'd break her neck.

By the time she reached the bottom, she felt a bit queenish. Her posture was even better. She was about to start humming when she realized someone else already was. It was a man's voice, and since there was little chance anyone had braved the storm, it had to be McKinnon. By the time she reached the parlor doors, he was singing. And she recognized the tune.

Let not yer cries call down the moon.
Let not yer prayers be led astray.
In the coachman's guise he'll grant yer boon,
And ye shall rue the price ye'll pay.

Bree peeked into the room. McKinnon was standing in the center of the large rug wearing his kilt again, damn him! Had he given her the dress so they'd match all day?

It was going to be a long day if she had to spend it with a guy who didn't have the decency to keep his knees together while wearing a skirt! She'd spent most of Christmas day looking away. But she forgot about all that while she watched Angeline danced around him, slowly, to match the pace of the melancholy tune first sung by the carriage driver. Her little hands were elegant as they stroked the air, like fine little paint brushes.

When he hit the chorus, the girl stepped in front of him and reached up, to place her hands against his chest. He stopped singing, looking confused. Angeline just smiled and gave him a nod. Then he started the chorus again while she...felt it.

> *"Take back the breath.*
> *Take back the sigh.*
> *Give not yer name.*
> *Yer boon deny.*
> *The Foolish Fire*
> *Comes not in twain.*
> *'Tis the coachman's lanterns*
> *Come for ye."*

The girls hands dropped away, but he caught one and held on, shaking his head. Then he reached down and placed his hand flat against the child's chest, between her collar bones. Then he nodded.

Bree frantically wiped tears from her eyes so she could see.

He was asking the child to sing. And when the tiny voice began to hum, Bree didn't know who was more surprised, McKinnon, herself, or Angeline.

The little girl pushed his hand away and replaced it with her own, like she couldn't quite believe the sound was coming from her own body. Then she began to dance, not taking the one hand from her chest.

She hummed the chorus, then when she reached a verse, she nodded to McKinnon again. He sang the words, while she continued humming.

"With hands of white and horses matched
He'll heigh thy love to broken heart.
Of measured dreams he'll grant behalf
And take from thee e'en the beggar's part."

McKinnon stepped forward and caught the girl up in his arms, then began waltzing around the room with her little feet dangling three feet off the ground.

She hummed louder. He sang all the while.

They spotted Bree in the doorway and McKinnon came to a dead stop, as did the song. She didn't know if the frown he gave her was for interrupting, or just breathing in general. But she pretended she didn't notice and stepped into the room.

"You're a natural, Mr. McKinnon. You've had a breakthrough all on your own. I can't imagine a better way to have coaxed her to try her voice."

Angeline was grinning. McKinnon lowered her to her feet and she hurried to Bree's side, taking her hand and leading Bree back to face McKinnon. The child tried to make him take Bree's hand, but he pulled away and shook his head.

Bree felt a little explosion of disappointment in her chest and the threat of more tears, but she would not give him the satisfaction of knowing he'd hurt her feelings.

"I'm sure Mr. McKinnon is not nearly so talented when dancing with full grown women, Angeline, so we really shouldn't embarrass him." Bree gave the jerk a snotty smile, then turned to go but the pan she carried got caught on something.

She'd completely forgotten she was carrying it. Then suddenly it was pulled out of her hand. When she whipped around, she found McKinnon coming toward her with murder in his eyes.

She stepped back like a wuss before she could remember she was a Colby and Colbys did not panic.

"Angeline, if ye will provide the music, I'm sure I can manage to drag Miss Colby around the room a few times without breaking all ten toes." Then, he spoke lower so the girl wouldn't hear. "Whether or not my touch will offend her is another matter."

A very enthusiastic humming began, still the same tune. Bree painted a smile on for the little girl and acted like she hadn't heard the last part. Then she was suddenly back in High School Ballroom Class trying to keep her partner from making them look bad. But the big lug was a lot harder to help than those sixteen-year-olds.

McKinnon grimaced. "Miss Colby, I assure you this will be much less painful if you allow me to lead the dance. Just relax into my arms... If you dare."

He wanted her to relax? Fine, she'd relax.

She laid her arms over his and leaned against the hand at her back. With part of her weight supported, her feet were light as feathers.

And they were waltzing!

Judging from the look on Angeline's face, it looked as lovely as it felt. And just as Bree had on the staircase, she felt regal, but more than that, it was working because she'd stopped fighting for control.

She forced her gaze up from McKinnon's neck to his eyes and realized he was as pleasantly surprised as she was. Of course he hid his surprise quickly and acted like he flew around the room all the time. But she could tell he didn't. He looked like a kid that knew how to ride a bike but couldn't get his hands on one very often. He smiled and winked at Angeline as they passed her again, but she could see the joy he was trying to hide. And even though his smile faded back to something polite when he looked at Bree, she could feel the excitement shooting through the arms that held hers up and allowed her feet to barely skim the floor.

Between the beginning of another chorus and the end, their smiles faded altogether. Her breath caught when she realized he'd looked at her just that way the night before. Just before she'd felt the need to run for her life.

She tried to pull her hand from his, but he held tight and started around the room again. She dropped her gaze to his neck, but could still see his face too clearly, so she looked at his chest. Staring at the breadth of it stole her breath away, and so she looked lower still.

Holy crap, what was she thinking?

She turned her head, found Angeline, and refused to look anywhere else.

The child's humming began to falter. She'd probably over-done it for her first day. Selfish as Bree was, she hadn't wanted the dancing to end. He wasn't smiling at her anymore, but he wasn't frowning either. At least not yet. She wanted to pretend, for another minute or two, that she wasn't his enemy.

Then suddenly, beneath her hands, came the low vibration of his humming. It was like having her arms wrapped around a volcano just as it started to erupt. Maybe he wasn't ready for it to end either.

Bree smiled again. She couldn't help it. She was in heaven. This was the romantic little moment she could share with her sisters and friends, a sweet memory of a charming man, the highlight of her trip. And if she could omit the fact that she might have to create an international incident to get home again, it was even more romantic—especially since he'd already kissed her. Maybe she could squish the memory of his kisses up against this one and pretend it had all happened the same day. And that she hadn't gotten spooked and run away.

She'd have to alter a few details, of course. Maybe she was in a little bar, in a tiny little village, and the master of nearby castle just stopped in for a pint with the locals. He'd noticed her sitting alone in a booth, looking over her little map of Scotland, wondering what to visit next.

And he'd granted a wish she hadn't remembered wishing for...

As they passed the velvet chaise they both turned to look at Angeline, resting against a cushion with her eyes closed, a smile still on her face. She and McKinnon shared a pleased smile, but it faded quickly. His humming ceased as he spun her out of his arms. By the time she stopped spinning, he was gone.

And her carriage turned back into a pumpkin.

CHAPTER THIRTEEN

The snow storm turned into freezing rain over night. And instead of the rain melting the snow, it covered it with a coating of clear frozen water. It was the coolest thing ever. It was the coldest thing ever, and the memory of nearly freezing to death was all it took to keep her from leaving the next morning.

She finally had to face the fact that she would never make her flight. She would have to use every penny she had in savings to get home. She would end up asking her dad for a loan and her mom would show up with a truck and moving boxes. It would be another six months before she'd have the guts to wrestle control of her life back from the well-meaning, but psycho woman and the cycle would start again.

But for now, she was done fighting Mother Nature and the nature of her mother. She'd make peace with Laird Gorgeous and try to figure out what that damned coachman was up to.

* * *

During the daytime, with Angeline to care for, to entertain, and to distract him, the tension in Heathcliff's chest lessened. But each night, as they tucked the child into her bed and took turns touching her one last time, McKinnon's blood would rise, unbidden.

But for the past two days, it had been different. The tension in his chest built not from distrust, but from anticipation. Even though it was preposterous to continue kissing a woman who was fearful where a kiss might lead, her lips were constantly in his thoughts. In an effort to remove them, he'd frequently sneak away to his tower room and draw a sketch of them, to transfer them from his mind onto paper. Unfortunately, they didn't stay where they were put. And the memories of their kisses were not nearly so easy to deal with.

That first kiss, which he stole from her only moments before he laid his accusations at her feet...

The Christmas Kiss, which he'd demanded in return for putting aside his suspicions—something he was trying to do before she'd even asked...

And now, another kiss was all he craved. More than food. More than a release from the frozen prison his home had become. He wanted it as much as he wanted this business with the coachman to be resolved. But as soon as it was resolved, she'd be gone.

It was a dark reality on the horizon. She'd be gone. He and Angeline would be left to carry on alone. He was no longer worried about communicating with the child. They seemed to be doing well whether or not Brianna was present. But he was a greedy bastard. He wanted them both.

It had been a mistake of course, to allow her to wear the clan colors. He'd had no idea it would affect him so, and while they'd danced together, he'd realized he would end as a begging puppy at her feet if he didn't get very far away from her. Then he'd hidden, like a coward, for the remainder of the day.

Dear Lord. What had he done, fallen in love with her?

There was only one way to find out. Another kiss. Only then would he ken for sure.

* * *

Bree was pissed.

Angeline had fallen asleep after dinner, and Heathcliff stuck his nose in a book and acted like he didn't want to talk to her if she didn't want to kiss him. At least she thought that was his problem. He hadn't spoken directly to her all day, and when she caught him looking at her, he was always staring at her lips. Then he'd stomp off like she shouldn't have caught him staring.

She told herself she wasn't going to get all physical with a guy who couldn't really trust her. But that was bullshit. She was scared to death.

She'd never slept with anyone before and she'd been determined to wait until she was married. But that wasn't the scary part. What really frightened her was the way Laird Gorgeous made her feel—like she could throw it all away for him. Like there was more passion in one kiss from him than in an hour of making out with David. Or anyone else.

She just couldn't give him the chance to ask her to because she already knew she'd say yes. And then her heart would be broken, and she'd be disappointed in herself for the rest of her life. Because she'd made that promise to that fourteen year old girl in the mirror. And that was one girl she hated to let down.

So, while she was dying to look her best, she had to dress like a grandma to try and keep him from wanting her. It was probably the hardest thing she'd ever done in her life. It went against every instinct, because who wouldn't want a guy who could walk down the streets of

Spokane, or anywhere else, and get his photo taken by every woman with a phone, and half the men.

Besides being handsome as sin, he had something else she couldn't put her finger on. Everything about him was masculine, powerful, perfect. It was like he was from another time and she was going to prove that impression was wrong. She had to find some proof that Heathcliff McKinnon was not from 1806.

Because the more time she spent with him and the more she'd seen of the kitchens, the more she'd started to worry. And the stupid popcorn popper had turned out to be a bed-warmer, with the year, 1797 on it!

For the past two days, every moment she hadn't spent with Angeline, she'd been methodically searching the castle. The only place she hadn't looked, besides the dungeons, was in the East Tower. If he'd made that tower his personal space, then of course that's where she'd discover the proof she was looking for. He'd have receipts and stuff. If the study was just another room for the tourists, then of course there would have been no proof there to find.

Walking around a dark castle at night was a pain in the butt. No wonder people used to rise with the sun and go to bed early. But those really weren't her hours. She couldn't wait to get back to electricity.

She lit three candles that stood in holes down the middle of a long tray. If one blew out, she wouldn't be sitting in the dark rubbing sticks or stones together; she'd have two more. Then she walked casually up the big staircase with the candles in one hand and her plaid nightgown in the other. She thought dressing as un-sexy as possible was probably a good idea, so she'd changed into her sweatpants and nightgown after they'd tucked Angeline in. When he'd given her the cold shoulder, it had been the excuse she needed to go back upstairs.

She snorted as she made her way toward the tower entrance. The sound of her own voice made it a little less scary, but not much. Candles didn't give off as much light as she'd expected—even three of them. So she imagined her safe space to be the circle of yellow light. Whatever was outside of that didn't matter, couldn't hurt her.

She tried the door. It opened right up. She grabbed the edge of it to slow the swing, so her candles wouldn't blow out.

There was a narrow walkway that curved, then a door beyond that. At the right end of the walkway were stairs going up. On the left, stairs going down. McKinnon's room must then occupy the center of the tower. She stepped forward and tried that door. It, too, opened easily, but she couldn't stop the door from swinging wide.

"Crap!" The candles flickered out in unison. "Damn it!" Her voice didn't help her at all.

"Perhaps I can be of help," Heathcliff growled from the hallway behind her.

She spun around to find the man basking in his own warm circle of light. It was brighter than hers had been, and he carried only one candle.

"Hurricane lamps are much more effective when walking...or sneaking. The glass protects and amplifies the flame."

Bree cleared her throat and stepped forward out of his private room. "How clever," she said and tried to step out of the tower, but he took a large step forward and blocked her path.

She couldn't tell if it was his expression, or just the way the light shined up on his face, but he looked menacing. She tried to hold her ground but he kept coming, herding her into his room.

She stepped backward quickly, to put some distance between them. He closed the door behind him. His expression never changed.

"I'm sorry I invaded your privacy," she said.

He said nothing.

She reached out and touched the cover on his bed. It was soft and rich. In fact, everything in his room looked luxurious—the bedding, the furniture, the art on the walls. There was a large painting that couldn't hang flat against the round wall—a fighting scene with fighting men in kilts atop huge white horses. Maybe it was the way the light bounced off everything, but none of it looked modern. She glanced at the desk that was built to fit the wall perfectly. There was an old-fashioned leather blotter and an inkwell. The pen wasn't a feather, but it looked old. Really, really old.

"I think I'm going to be sick," she said and looked around for a garbage can. Of course there wasn't one, which only made her sicker.

"Are ye so suddenly ill, then?" He lifted his light to look at her better, but he looked doubtful.

"I need to sit down." She used his little stool to climb up on his bed and sat down carefully.

"Since I'm certain ye didna come here to seduce me..." He just left the words hanging. She really had no choice but to confess before he started thinking she'd come to rob the place.

"I was looking for a receipt or something, okay? Something with the date on it."

"Did I not show ye enough envelopes with the date written upon them?"

"Not written. I just need to find something stamped. Computerized. Official."

"So that is today's tack, is it? Ye wish to convince me that the year is far into the future. But why? Hope ye I will say so before a judge, so I might be found insane?

Is that the best plan you and yer coachman could think of? Because I will never believe yer rantings."

She laughed. "Ranting. *I'm* ranting. *I'm* the one who's crazy?"

She considered it for a minute. She'd been scooped up by a guy in a sleigh, but he'd known the name of the tour company. He'd known the guy who rented her the car. He didn't seem to think she was crazy. But then again, the guy, his sleigh, and his horses had disappeared damned fast.

Maybe it wasn't a question of crazy. Maybe it was a question of *magic.*

Holy crap! "Maybe you should tell me more about your grandma," she said.

Heathcliff stared at her for so long, she wondered if time had frozen. But then she noticed the flicker of his candle. Still, it didn't mean she hadn't entered a real Twilight Zone.

Finally, he blinked and walked to the nightstand where he set his light down. When he turned to face her, he towered above her, even though she sat on his insanely high bed.

"I believe I know what ye're about to say, lass, and I'm warning ye to reconsider. I won't countenance an insult to me grandmother."

"Well, if you know what I'm thinking, I don't need to say it. But you have to admit something crazy is going on here and *I'm* not crazy." She'd like to claim that crazy didn't run in her family, but she wasn't too sure about her mother.

"I wouldna be so certain," he growled.

Her jaw hit the floor, but before she had time to recover, the room lit up brilliantly like someone had found a light switch. It was lightening, flashing, lighting up the white horses in the painting. Half a second later came the crack and boom of thunder that lit up her bones as she flew off the bed and into Heathcliff's arms.

He grabbed her tight to sooth her shaking, then threw back his head and laughed; he was shaking too.

It took a minute for her eyes to adjust back to the near-darkness, and when they did, Heathcliff's eyes were boring into hers. His smile was gone. His hands slid across her back as he pulled her tight...and kissed her.

She guessed, by the way he was kissing her, the granny nightgown hadn't worked. But then, she hadn't really wanted it to. And the most primal feminine side of her was thrilled that he found her desirable in spite of everything. She let that side of her enjoy his kiss while the rational side of her stood back and shrieked, *Hello. He insulted us!*

Maybe she wasn't so mentally balanced after all.

McKinnon pulled back and pressed his forehead to hers. She heard him say *damn* under his breath, and not in a *hot damn* kind of way.

Her primal feminine ego took a nose dive.

"Wish you wouldn't have kissed the crazy chick, huh?" She pushed out of his arms and headed for the door. "Well, don't worry about it, sport. She wishes she hadn't kissed you either."

He cleared his throat. "I meant nothing of the sort, lass."

He didn't sound convincing at all.

She grabbed the latch and turned to face him, but she couldn't quite manage a carefree smile.

"It's pretty silly for me to hang around and argue with you until New Year's Eve. I'll just pack my stuff and take off in the morning."

"Lass, wait."

She was grateful for easy-opening doors that let her get away quickly. When the tower door shut behind her, she'd taken a few steps before she realized she'd been plunged into the darkness again. But it didn't matter. Her bedroom was just down the hall. She'd see the firelight under the door in a second or two.

The hallway suddenly lit up behind her, but she didn't turn.

"I don't need your light, thanks. I'm fine." She picked up the pace, but he grabbed her arm and forced her to stop. She wouldn't look at him, no matter how he tried to make her.

"Brianna. Please. I must know what ye meant. What is it ye plan to take off in the morning?"

Oh please. What was he hoping for, a strip tease?

"Take off means *go, leave, depart*. I'll be out of your hair as soon as the sun comes up. I'll tell Angeline goodbye. I won't run out on her without saying a word."

"Ye mean to *leave*?"

She nodded once but couldn't face him. He probably looked relieved, and that would only hurt her feelings worse.

Slowly, finger by finger, he let go of her arm.

She walked as calmly as possible toward her room, hoping he couldn't tell she was dragging her heart behind her.

CHAPTER FOURTEEN

Once Brianna was in her room, Heathcliff returned to his.

He removed his boots and his cravat, and his coat. Then, without so much as considering the wisdom of it, without considering anything at all, he simply took up the blankets from his bed and dragged them out of the tower and down the hallway where he set his candle on a table next to a figurine. He wrapped the tale of his plaid and his mass of blankets around himself, then sat on the floor with his back against her bedchamber door.

There.

Leave? Of course she could leave—over his dead and frozen body. He didn't care for her odds, however, since the door was warm at his back and heat slipped out from beneath it.

As he sat in the soft glow of the candle, he thought about the kiss—the kiss that made it quite clear to him that he had, in fact, fallen in love with the woman. He'd reacted badly to the news, though, hadn't he? Of course, she'd reacted badly to his reaction. So perhaps the lass felt the same about him. The fact that she was quite mad had nothing at all to do with it.

But just how mad was she?

If something unnatural happened around the castle while Grandmother was still alive, none would blink an eye. But the old woman was gone and all excitement had ceased. Hadn't it?

If he considered the past few days, looking for unnatural happenings, he would have to admit that the child's arrival had been a bit queer. Welcomed, but queer.

The woman's arrival of course. The quick disappearance of the coachman along with his four-in-hand. But he'd been so distracted by the...*underthings* perched on Brianna's head that he mightn't have noticed the house catching fire for a moment or two—so the man's departure did not signify.

The storm. A more violent winter he could never remember, especially considering the wee avalanche that might well have taken his life. He thanked God there had been someone about to help him.

Suspecting a child had been a bit unnatural on his part—

But wait! The avalanche. The distraction a moment before.

The murmur. He'd forgotten about the murmur—his words tossed back at him! *The pair of ye should be grateful for one another.*

Heathcliff closed his eyes and let his head rest against the wood at his back. How had he forgotten about the voice? The disembodied voice?

He wished there was another Muir Witch nearby upon whom he might call for advice. But all of those who had once lived among his clan were gone. He was the only one left with any Muir blood—

He was the only one left.

He was the only one left!

Heathcliff's heart jumped from the frightening idea he'd found huddled in the recesses of his mind. He turned over his forearm and looked at the large blue vein through which his Muir blood ran. Brianna believed something unnatural was underfoot. Could *he* be that something?

He'd wished for a family a hundred times before. Why did a child appear in his life now? He'd wanted a wife, and if he'd have been able to fashion a woman to order, he'd have preferred a woman he could love, first and fore. Angelic hair? Lovely blue eyes? Were they not part of many a fantasy that had slipped into his dreams, back when he'd allowed himself to dream?

And the storm? Had he conjured it somehow, when he'd been standing at his window that night, wishing for the ability to communicate with his new child? Or had it been a work of Nature? Perhaps it had, but once it arrived, had it remained because it helped him to keep the woman in his home?

Had he summoned a voice from a child who had none? It had taken but a touch from his hand...

God forgive him! He wanted to stand and pace the hallway; he could barely sit still with such thoughts flying through his skull—but he dared not. What if such unnatural power sat upon his shoulder, ready to bring about his will with barely a thought? No, he dared not give in to the temptation to test it. He was a God-fearing man, for pity sakes.

His mind wandered back down the hall to his tower room. As disappointed as he'd been in finding her sneaking where she'd promised not to go, he'd found it impossible not to move to the side of the bed. She sat upon it so casually, she couldn't have known how it had affected him. The sight of her there would likely greet him each and every night when he retired!

He'd set aside his candle, not trusting himself with a dangerous flame when his hands were shaking so. He'd hardly noticed the discussion, focused as he was on taking that kiss. He'd needed that kiss. He'd been determined to know, once and for certain, if he were in love, or if he were only infatuated with her.

He'd insulted her. Possibly more than once with his inattention. And then he'd gotten what he'd come for. She'd popped off the bed and into his arms as if he'd summoned her to him.

As if he'd conjured the lightning to encourage her into his arms.

Dear God!

Heathcliff buried his face in his hands and began to pray.

The next thing he remembered was waking on the floor, cold and stiff, with a feather light touch on his cheek. He shivered as he sat up and gathered his blankets tight around him.

The child stood before him with a decidedly heartbroken look upon her face.

"Fear not, Angeline. I'll not allow Miss Colby to abandon us." He rolled his shoulders and prepared to stand.

Angeline's bottom lip caught his attention as it was both protruding and quivering, so Heathcliff rolled onto a knee and reached for her.

"There, there, my cherub. Dinna greet. Go back inside and fetch Miss Colby. We'll sort it all out."

He thanked God Brianna would be able to decipher what had upset the child so. He hoped the cold hadn't made her ill. When he got to his feet, however, Angeline wrapped her arms around his legs.

And finally he understood. Brianna was gone.

CHAPTER FIFTEEN

When Bree woke up and it was still dark, her primal feminine side suggested she go back to sleep and pretend she and Heathcliff hadn't had a falling out. But since her PF had been the one to get carried away and embarrass the hell out of her last night, Bree wasn't listening.

Heathcliff didn't want her there. If he believed the note, she was a threat to him and his little girl. She was a threat to his sanity if he really believed the year was 1806. He couldn't possibly relax with the clock ticking down to New Year's Eve, but he let her stay anyway. Why? Because he knew how sexy he was and thought there was a chance she'd mess around with him, of course. It was probably the only reason he was allowing her to stay—just in case she decided to cave in.

He sure didn't need Bree in order to communicate with Angeline.

It had been a mistake to sneak into his room.

"I'm certain ye didna come here to seduce me..." And she was certain he wasn't too happy about that.

Well, every girl had been in that position by the time she was seventeen or eighteen at least. *Sleep with me or go home.* So she was going home. At least she hoped she was going home.

When she found her way out through the gatehouse, the weather got pretty wild. She couldn't believe it was still storming! It had been going at it hard for four or five days straight! But this time she was prepared. Since there was no way she was going to be able to drag her suitcase down the snowy road, she'd put on just about everything she had. Only this time, she used a sweater for a hat and kept her underwear on her butt where it belonged. She was also starting out with nice, water-tight rainboots. Staying warm would be easy enough—she only had to tough it out until she got to the inn Heathcliff claimed was at the bottom of the hill. She just hoped she'd be able to see it through the blowing snow.

Man, it was going to be nice to see a new face.

It was the twenty-ninth. She should have been on a plane that morning. She would have settled for a car, but Heathcliff swore he didn't have a vehicle. And if someone pulled up in a horse drawn sleigh, even if he had a nice white beard and wore red velvet, she wouldn't get in.

She trudged on. As long as she was going downhill, she was going in the right direction, out of the Twilight Zone. She kept her weight centered over her boots so she didn't slip on the icy patches. Cute waterproof boots? Yes. Traction? Not so much.

A wolf howled. A real live wolf! How crazy was that?

She stopped walking. Oh, how stupid was she? Of course there would be wolves. Wild wolves, with no fence or TV screen between her and them. The castle was in the hills, away from town, away from people. And if she were a wolf, she'd either be snuggled in a den or out looking for food. Since she was feeling pretty foodie, she got moving, only a lot faster than before.

Oh, she was an idiot. When had her pride made her so blind?

"Well, maybe only when men were involved," she said, to hear her own voice. She'd been too proud to admit that her relationship with David wasn't the fairytale romance she'd dreamed of as a teen. Now she was too proud to tell Laird Gorgeous that she didn't really want to go away and never see him again. Too proud to tell him that she was afraid of his kisses because they were just too wonderful. That she was afraid she'd handed her heart over to him when he'd placed his hand on Angeline's chest and invited her to hum. When he'd made her feel like a princess waltzing with a prince, and a desirable woman when she was dressed like her grandma.

And now she might end up being a very proud, but very dead American whose bones wouldn't be discovered until spring.

But wouldn't wolves eat bones too?

She passed a big bush with a bare branch sticking out the top. It looked like a rabbit. Maybe the wolves were hunting rabbits.

The ground leveled out. She might be close to the inn! And people. And noises. And cars. And things that probably made wolves run back into the forest.

"Hello!" It had been a lot easier to walk downhill. The snow was so deep now it spilled over the tops of her boots, but she was almost there. "Please, let me be close," she muttered. "Hello," she hollered again. Every minute she walked without hearing a howl, her hope grew. It was like counting the seconds between lightning and thunder. She was moving farther away!

A large shape darkened as she got near. It was a big bush with a familiar branch sticking out of it. Holy crap! She'd been walking in circles! She looked down, searching for her own footprints. They were barely visible. The huge paw prints, which followed alongside them, were much fresher.

A wolf howled, this time clearer than ever before. But with the swirling snow, she couldn't tell from which direction it had come.

If she ran, would they just be chasing each other until she couldn't keep up?

To her left was dense growth. To her right lay a rocky ledge. The memory of that half-frozen stream kept her from trying that way. She had to be standing in the middle of the road. She just had to be. So how had she gone in circles?

Frenzied growling erupted in the trees, like dogs fighting. Fear helped propel her down the road like a rock from a slingshot. She'd be an idiot to stand around arguing with herself when she could put some distance between her and the animals. So she ran. She watched her footprints, for the moment when they'd veer off to the left, but they continued straight. It was madness. If she kept going, would she be circling around to face the wolves again? She had to change course! She had to head left!

The realization that freezing to death in a ditch was preferable to being torn apart by fangs was enough to make up her mind. She hurried to the rocks and looked for a path to take, but just beyond the rocks were twisted, thorny branches she couldn't possibly work her way through. She ran farther down the road and looked again. No good. A straight drop off. No telling how far the drop to the snow was, or what was underneath it.

She turned back toward the road just as a large black beast ran at her.

She screamed. It reared and screamed back.

A horse!

"Brianna!"

The animal turned and mounted on the back was Heathcliff. Behind him was a huge white wolf with blood dripping out of its nose and mouth, splattering in an arc as the horse turned. Though it was slung behind the saddle and not moving, the eyes still looked alive. The tongue wavered as blood dripped off the edge.

Instinctively, she backed away.

Heathcliff's hand shot out and grabbed the front of her coat just as her right foot slipped off the ledge. She felt herself lifted into the air and dropped onto the man's lap before the echo of her gasp died away.

"Brianna," he shouted again. "Brianna. Lass. Finally. Oh, Brianna." He let go of her coat and wrapped his arms around her, squeezing the air out of her lungs. Her shock was so complete, she couldn't seem to lift her arms to hug him back.

She twisted so she could breathe again. "I can't believe you came after me," she said against the sleeve of his coat. The dark, stiff fur brought a tingle to her numb chin.

He pulled back and looked at her. Their faces were only inches apart.

"Brianna. My heart. I canna believe ye sneaked by me. How can you believe I'd let ye leave?"

"I just assumed—"

"Oh, forgive me, lass. I believed ye were past arguin' last eve, so I saved my arguin' for this morn. Only ye were gone. Surely, when ye saw I'd planted my backside before yer door, ye kenned I wanted ye to stay."

She bit her lips. Yeah, she'd gotten the message. He didn't want her to get away, but she thought it was only because he was, well, horny. It wasn't something she wanted to admit out loud though.

And he'd come after her, in the storm, on a freaking horse. And he'd killed the wolf she'd been trying to outrun.

"That wolf is huge! I can't believe you killed it."

He sighed and rolled his eyes. "Huge. Real. Live. And yes, I killed it. And no, we're not going to eat it."

"Then why did you keep it?"

He looked away, like he was embarrassed. "If there were others about, which I'm sure there are, I can toss them the carcass and get away, aye?"

Well, that was reasonable. But then why would he be embarrassed?

"What aren't you telling me?"

She wanted him to look at her again, so their faces would be close again. After the adrenaline fest she'd just had, a kiss sounded pretty good, whether it gave him the wrong idea or not.

"I wanted to impress ye, Brianna Colby. I want to win yer heart, as ye've won mine. I want ye to come back. And stay."

A twig snapped. It wasn't loud, but to her ears, it sounded like a gunshot.

Heathcliff turned the horse and got it moving without showing any of the panic she felt. But of course he wouldn't be worried. He'd already killed one without getting hardly any blood on him at all. The thought made her shiver.

She figured they were headed in the right direction because the thick forest was now on their right, the edge of the drop off on their left. After a few minutes, she relaxed. It was nice not having to trudge back up the mountain in the snow, but she felt sorry for the horse.

"Brianna, love. There is something ye should know. Something I realized last night, after... Well, after."

Bree looked at her hands and waited. This was where he was going to tell her that he was gay or something. One of those "I like you alot, but" moments. She'd had a lot of those with David.

"I've said my grandmother was thought to be a witch."

That got her attention. She looked up at him then. He was biting his lip, glancing at her, then back at the road.

If she said anything, he'd probably never get the words out, so she waited.

"I fear that I, too... That I too might be a witch."

Bree snorted. "Men aren't witches, though. They're warlocks, right?"

It was a joke. It had to be a joke. She kept waiting for him to smile, but he didn't.

"Males can be witches, lass. For many a man was killed for being such not long ago."

Well, *not long ago* to a Brit was a lot longer than *not long ago* to an American. Their history went back millennia. But why would he say something like that? Did he want to creep her out so she'd go away? If so, why not just leave her to the wolves? Why come after her? She didn't get it.

"I don't get it," she said aloud.

"Think on it, Brianna. I've wanted a family and here I've had one dropped in me lap. The storm keeps you from leavin' me. The lightening brought ye into me arms last eve so I could have the kiss I'd come for."

"You think you can control the weather?" She pushed aside the fact that she'd imagined a mean spirited fairy pushing her car off the road.

"I do, lass. And I believe it now more than I did before. Listen. The wind and snow have settled since we turned for home, have they not?"

The wind had nearly stopped. A little caress crossed her face, shook a branch here and there along the path, but it wasn't blowing anymore. And there were sounds now. Some winter-tough birds chattered in the trees. The temperature had even come up. The clouds looked like they'd backed off, even though they still didn't let any sunshine through.

"You think you stopped the storm?" She looked up into his eyes, looking for signs of crazy. Surely she'd be able to tell if he was nuts. But he looked back at her, unflinching. His brown eyes were a lot lighter outside than they were inside his castle, a lot easier to read.

He believed it. He thought he could control the weather. And it made her sad.

"Shall we test it?" The corner of his mouth lifted. His eyes jumped with excitement.

If he tested it, and it didn't work, would he take it badly? If he did, would she want to stand by his side and help him through it?

Why not? She'd already missed her flight. She had a mother of a storm to blame for not calling home yet. There was nothing she could do at the moment.

"Yes," she said. "But how can you test it?"

He grinned. Like a boy taking a new airplane out of the package, getting ready to launch it.

"I believe the storm exists to keep you at the castle." He turned the horse around.

The beast hadn't taken three steps before the wind picked up again, like it was trying to blow them back up the hill. The snow joined in, slapping them in the face. The sweater was blown from her head. He didn't seem to think it was worth stopping for.

"Okay! Okay, let's go back."

"Do ye believe me, lass?" He'd yelled to be heard above the wind whistling around them, and she was sitting on his lap.

"Yes! Turn us around," she said, but she didn't really believe—couldn't really believe.

The horse turned again, but the storm didn't stop. She held her breath, feeling each step the horse took, wanting to let herself fall apart. It was all just too crazy. It was a good thing Angeline was so young she didn't realize that the world around her had gone nuts.

Angeline!

She turned to ask Heathcliff what he'd done with the little girl and noticed she didn't need to yell. The storm had fizzled out again.

But there is no such thing as witches.

Then the light dawned. "You're doing this," she said.

"That is what I've been trying to tell ye, aye?"

She shook her head. "No. I mean, you're doing this. You've got wind machines and snow machines or something. You've done this on purpose. You're in on the joke, with the coachman. This is all a set up. Why didn't I see it before? I knew I shouldn't trust you."

Heathcliff frowned and shook his head. He held on tighter, like he thought she might jump down and run. Which was just what she would do, if she had a car to run to.

"Nay, lass. Let us get inside and get settled. Jump to no conclusions. I dinna care for the way your mind is turning. Of course ye should trust me."

Bree looked up and realized they were about to reach the gatehouse. That fast? She'd been walking for a long time, but apparently she'd been walking in circles for longer than she'd thought.

After a little hesitation, he helped her slide off then jumped down himself. He walked his horse through the small, low opening that was probably only meant for people. She shivered, but not from the cold. She no longer felt like she knew the guy walking behind her.

CHAPTER SIXTEEN

———✦———

Heathcliff had mucked it up and mucked it up good.

Brianna had given him no chance at conversation. She'd latched onto the child and was using Angeline as a shield between them. For the rest of the day, they'd been unable to speak freely.

But Angeline had yawned herself to sleep while Brianna told the tale of a woman who was held prisoner in a castle by a beast. It ended well for Heathcliff, however, when in the end, the beast turned into a handsome prince and was exonerated.

Brianna had quickly claimed it was her least favorite story of all time.

"Then why did ye tell it?" He laughed and took the cherub up the stairs. When Brianna invited him to leave the room so she could retire, he scooped her up in his arms and strode from the room with her.

"'Tis what any self-respecting beast would do, aye?" He carried her down the stairs and back to the parlor. "We will have this out, Brianna. Now. The only part of it ye'll be choosin' is whether or not ye shall be tied to a chair or sitting comfortably.

She folded her arms and sat on the chaise.

"That's fine, then," he said, but kept a close eye whilst he stoked the fire.

He dropped a bit of plaid wool over her shoulders, then sat down at the opposite end of the lounge. She could not complain there wasn't sufficient room between them.

"So. Ye doona believe in witches?"

She shook her head and rolled her eyes.

"Neither do I."

Her head whipped to the side. At least he had her attention.

"The back of a horse was hardly the place for this conversation. My apologies."

She turned and brought a knee up onto the couch so she could face him full on, but still, she didn't speak.

"I thought perhaps I'd done something magical when Angeline began to hum."

She smiled briefly.

"And you saw what happened with the weather."

She gave him an evil eye. He laughed.

"But I'll admit I've tried to make other things happen. Make things move. And I felt rather foolish when naught came of it. For instance, I canna get ye to come to my end of the couch now, can I?"

She smiled and shook her head.

"Well, then. I suppose I'm not a witch after all. But there is no doubt about it. Something unnatural is happening here, as ye said. And I thought if ye decided to stay with me, forever, that it only right to warn ye of the possibility that my blood might be a bit...tainted."

Her brows rose. She shook her head. She braced herself as if preparing to run.

"Forever? What are you talking about?"

He leaned forward and willed her to believe him sincere.

"I love ye, Brianna Colby. Rain, shine, snow, wind. It has naught to do with the weather. Naught to do with holidays or notes written by lunatics. Marry me. Stay with me. Go where I go. Be with me always. *Marry me.*"

She did not run, fortunately.

But she did laugh.

She laughed for a good long while, truth be told, until he decided it would have been kinder of her to run away.

"I'm being punked," she said. "I get it now." Her smile faded a bit, turned a little sad. "My family? My so-called friends? Who's behind it? I really don't know anyone who could afford it, but wow. Just...wow."

"Lass. What are ye sayin'? If ye didna notice, I've just proposed marriage. I thought I was speakin' English when I did so, but perhaps I'm mistaken."

"Oh, I heard you." She waved a dismissive hand and got to her feet. "So what's supposed to happen at midnight on New Year's Eve? Huh? Everyone going to burst through the door? Balloons going to drop from the ceiling

She tipped her head and looked at the rafters, then back at him.

"I'll tell you what. If this little conversation hasn't been caught on tape, you're secret is safe with me. I'll keep going along with it. We've got what? Two full days left?"

He could only stare at her. Was the difference in language so great then? Did she not understand what he'd offered? Because he certainly had no ken of her meaning.

Punked? What was punked?

But he didn't feel much like looking more the fool, so he didn't ask.

"I'm relieved, really," she was saying, bringing him back to the conversation. "I was starting to believe I was actually in 1806. And your castle really is amazing."

He bowed his head to acknowledge the compliment, but he still did not trust his tongue.

"You know where they screwed up though?"

He shook his head. He didn't understand the question, but he could at least tell it was a question.

"You."

"Me?" His voice did not break with the emotions roiling in his chest, for which he was grateful.

"Yeah. You. You were too good to be true. Right from the beginning. Too handsome. Too..." She took a slow breath and let it out in a rush. "Too perfect."

She grimaced and turned away, but not before he noticed her blush. At least she found him pleasant to look upon. But she couldn't have had feelings for him, or surely she wouldn't have laughed at his proposal.

A pleasant facade was all he could muster then. His insides felt as if they were being hollowed out, like a pumpkin.

By the time he'd escorted her up the stairs and to her chamber door, he had decided on his parting words. If they kept her from sleeping, so be it.

"Goodnight, Mr. McKinnon." Her smile was bright, but she was nervous.

"Just a moment," he said.

She placed her hand on the latch, but did not open the door. Prepared to run, as always.

"Yer mistaken about a few things."

"Oh?" Her confidence was slipping fast. Her grip in the latch tightened. She probably thought he was going to kiss her. But they were beyond that.

He reached out and handed her the walking candle.

"I am nay, nor have I been, conspiring with anyone to, uh, punk ye. I fear no one bursting through my door at midnight on New Year's Eve, save a villainous coachman, and I'd nay fear him but I have a child to protect. When my servants return, I will arrange transportation for ye, wherever ye care to go. The year is 1806. And it's Heathcliff."

He turned and stepped away, but he heard her gasp over the clacking of his boots.

"Then you really—"

He spun on his heel but didn't smile. "Yes. I really." Then he spun back and walked into the darkness.

Heathcliff reached for the door of his tower room, but he could not face the memory of her sitting on his bed. Not just yet, anyway. He was exhausted, to be sure. But not the kind of fatigue that would help him sleep anytime soon. So he turned right and climbed to the top of the tower. A little cold air and a bit of perspective was in order.

Perhaps the moon would ken how a man might fall *out* of love with a woman.

* * *

Bree couldn't seem to make herself open the door and go inside. Angeline was in there. Angeline, to whom she shouldn't be getting more attached because her daddy was crazy. He was lying about the year. He was wrong to think he could have fallen in love with someone after just a week. She'd been with David for a year and a half and had to work damn hard to get him to love her. Love just couldn't come that easily.

Could it?

She shook her head and slid down the door, found herself sitting where she'd found Heathcliff just that morning, trying to tell her that he didn't want her to go. Because he...loved her?

Holy crap! Was he telling the truth?

Was it just David that made love so difficult? Maybe instead of Bree being hard to love, it was just that David was all wrong for her. She'd tried so hard to make herself fit his life, like a puzzle piece that left gaps; she thought all she needed was to fill in those gaps. But she belonged to a different puzzle.

Maybe it was possible to fall in love in a week.

Oh, she was an idiot. Of course it was possible—she'd done it herself! Why else would her heart have broken when she thought she was being punked?

Her feet were moving toward the tower before she realized she'd made a decision, headed into the dark without caring if her candle went out. She wasn't afraid of shadows as much as she was afraid it was too late. Maybe she'd run away from him one too many times.

Her yellow circle of light fell on the tower door covered with gnarly celtic knots. She pulled, then sighed in relief. He hadn't locked her out. She stepped across the walkway and was glad the door to his room was smoother. She knocked quickly—for fear of chickening out.

Three times.

She took a deep breath and got ready to apologize.

He didn't answer.

She knocked again.

No movement. No way was he already asleep. She'd give him one last chance. If he didn't hear her knock the third time, then it wasn't meant to be. Maybe this wasn't her puzzle either. Maybe Heathcliff needed a puzzle piece from 1806!

She knocked. Hard.

Nothing.

She smashed her ear against the door, to see if she could hear him snoring. There was nothing. He knew she was there, and he didn't care. He'd made his decision.

The way back to Angeline's door was better lit, if only from her red face.

* * *

Heathcliff found his perspective on the roof. Looking down upon his land, snow-covered as it was, he realized that the world was too lonely a place to walk it alone. Since the moon was nowhere in sight, he got no advice from that quarter. He would simply be forced to go on loving his mad-as-a-hatter American who believed she was from the future.

She believed something else as well—he couldn't fathom how he'd missed it all this time—she believed he didna love her because she believed no one could.

Well, he'd just have to convince her. He had two entire days in which to do so. And if he could not... Well, then, he'd just have to keep on trying, after they were finished chasing the coachman out of their lives.

The servants would return. She'd appreciate the activity, he was sure. And the three of them could put their unnatural holiday behind them.

"Come, storm. Do yer worst. Keep the lass by my side until I can win her," he said.

Just in case.

CHAPTER SEVENTEEN

Although he had every right to feel insulted the next day, it was Brianna who acted so. She'd gotten quite the large bee in her bonnet, and there seemed to be no way to get it out. She smiled at Angeline each and every time the lassie looked in her direction, but she had no smile for him. And nary a word.

Her eyes were rimmed with red. It should have given him some solace that she'd wept a bit, but it only frustrated him for wanting to console her. He believed in his bones she loved him, for she'd already admitted she believed him to be perfect. Too good to be true, she'd said.

The memory forced a smile to his face. He cleared his throat.

"I thought, since we havna much time left," he began, hoping he might win her attention. But alas, she made no indication she could hear him at all. "I thought perhaps the pair of us can get to know one another a wee bit better. Perhaps ye can tell me what it's like, where ye're from. The year I mean. Is there anything of the future that might be helpful for me to know beforehand?"

She smiled. A good sign, that. But then she barked out a laugh that wasna flattering for her and didna bode

well for him. He was almost relieved when she stood and
left the room.

But he wouldna give up. A smile was a smile. And
silence could be broken.

* * *

That night Bree took a book from Heathcliff's
library and swore she wasn't going to give him the time
of day. She stayed in a blue wing-backed chair on the far
side of the room so he'd have no reason to wonder where
she was and a good reason to give her some privacy. She
kept her back at an angle to the fire so she'd have enough
light to see the words. And every few minutes, she had to
remember to turn the page, so he would think she was
actually reading the damn thing.

She thought it was a romance. The title said
something about the birds and the bees. It turned out to
be a farmer's guide. And even worse, the letters were all
messed up on some of the words. If she skimmed and
read fast, her mind kind of filled in the blanks and she
understood a little bit. But her mind wasn't working all
that fast. It kept stalling, getting distracted by how
absolutely pissed she was.

Of course she wasn't pissed, she was hurt. But
pissed was a lot easier to pull off because she wasn't
going to walk around sniffling, and she'd be damned if
she was going to lock herself in that bedroom for two
days. So pissed worked.

She hadn't spoken to him all afternoon. She'd gone
through the library looking at every publication date she
could find. But she eventually gave up hope. She was,
quite possibly, spending her holiday in 1806 Scotland
and she wasn't freaking out because it was the second
best explanation if she was not being punked. It would be
a relief, having so much explained and accounted for.

And she had to admit, she would be relieved that Heathcliff wasn't actually insane.

There were a lot of things it didn't explain, though—like Angeline.

The girl knew American Sign Language. *American.* And it sure as hell wasn't around in 1806. And the French version? Half of that made no sense in English. Was the girl from the future too?

Oh, wow. She was not even going to suggest that to Heathcliff. He was going to freak out enough if she ever came up with proof she was from 2012. And if the coachman showed up with her handbag...

Crap was going to hit the fan at midnight. She could feel it. And if she ended up in a different century, then there was no sense letting Heathcliff know how she felt about him. It would only make it harder on them both.

While she scoured the library, Laird Gorgeous had wandered around the castle holding Angeline's hand. The child hadn't seemed to notice there was anything wrong, so she continued with the silent treatment. In fact, she only spoke when it was time to put Angeline to bed. Since *Goodnight Moon* had become the girl's favorite story, Bree recited it again from memory, then kissed the little girl and said goodnight.

McKinnon asked what a balloon was. She walked out of the room as if she hadn't heard him.

"Sucks to be you," she whispered as she headed for the stairs.

"I heard that." He sounded so smug. What did he think, that if she spoke to him the silent treatment would end?

What an amateur.

* * *

"You forgot to turn the page," he said, from his spot on the chaise. He'd turned the couch so it faced her, like he thought it would make her uncomfortable to know she was being watched. Silly man.

She was back in her gnawed-off jeans, a button-up shirt, and a cardigan. She knew that most of the time, he was just staring at the two inches of her calves that were visible above her rain boots. Apparently, showing flesh wasn't proper. But she couldn't just let him get away with staring at her all night.

She closed her book. He put a foot on the floor. What did he think, she was suddenly going to run out into the snow and disappear? She turned, so he could have a nice view of her profile while she stripped off the cardigan. She could hear him swallow from twelve feet away. Not giggling was the hardest thing she'd done all day.

She sat down again and opened her book. Flipped through a few pages as if she was trying to find her place, then settled in to read again.

"The book is upside down," he said.

But it wasn't. She just ignored him.

Did he think this was strip poker? That she'd shed another piece of clothing every time he caught her doing something dumb?

She turned her head and gave him the once over. Of course that's what he thought! She snorted and went back to reading. He started fidgeting with his fingers.

"I'm sorry if my proposal frightened ye."

She didn't even blink.

"I am content to woo and win ye at a slower pace, if that would put ye at ease."

She turned the page.

"I beg your forgiveness in any case."

His brogue stirred her insides, so she decided to stir his. She put a toe to heel and pried off one boot. She could hear him breathing, feel him watching. She slipped it off, wiggled her toes, then took of the other. She straightened her ankle socks, then went back to reading.

"There is a large insect in yer hair," he said.

Without looking at him, she leaned down, picked up a boot, and chucked it at him as hard as she could. Then she went back to reading. Words. She was pretty sure there were words on the page. She just couldn't see them.

He jumped out of his seat. She jumped out of her skin. He ran toward her and she pulled up her leg in self-defense, than started slapping at him, doggy-paddle-style.

"Be still. I'll remove it," he grumbled, trying to stop her hands.

"Remove what?" she yelled.

"The insect, ye contrary, fractious woman!"

Bree screamed, then whimpered while trying to hold still enough for the creature to be caught.

"I have it," McKinnon claimed, then stomped to the fire and tossed something in—or pretended to. He turned to her. "It was only a beetle. Ye were nay harmed." He took a deep breath. Then another. "Ye are far too precious for me to allow ye to be harmed, lass."

She realized that last part had nothing to do with the bug, and she suddenly felt herself falling to pieces. She was caught off guard, and the self-pity she loathed snuck in and took her by surprise. And she burst into tears like she had the first time he'd left her in the water closet.

He walked toward her, his hands out like he was walking up to a skittish horse, like he wanted to comfort her.

"Don't touch me," she said. She didn't need his comfort.

He kept coming. She thought crying would have scared him away.

"I said, don't touch me!"

Then he did. He tried to comb his fingers through her hair. She swatted at his hand, but it just came back. She jumped off the chair and started slapping him with both hands again.

Okay, so maybe she could have hit him harder, but she didn't really want to hurt him. She just wanted him to stop touching her! She only had to get through one more day in this oversized loony bin and she could go home and forget about him. Forget about Scotland and the whole crazy nightmare. She just had to get through one more day! She just had to stay on her side of the room for 24 more hours.

She wiped her nose on her sleeve because she had nothing else. Then she slapped the tears from her cheeks and pointed at the chaise. "Get back on your side of the room and forget I'm here!"

He pulled her against his chest, trapping her hands between their bodies. Looking down into her face, he whispered, "I doona wish to forget, lass. Heaven help me, but I doona."

And there he was, stealing another kiss. He deserved to get his face wet.

His hand came up behind her head, to let her know that this time, it might take a while. As soon as he let up, she was going to argue with him, tell him to keep his lips to himself. But he didn't let up for a good long while. And when he did, she forgot what she was going to say.

He scooped up her legs and carried her back to the chaise.

Oh, boy was he going to be disappointed when she told him *no*. Her dates usually were. Some even got pretty pissed, but she'd already dealt with McKinnon's angry side. He wasn't such a badass.

He laid her on the velvet, then sat down and kicked off his boots.

She opened her mouth to tell him he might not want to bother, but he laid a finger across her lips. The gentle touch felt like another kiss and when he removed it, she sat very still and waited for him to do it again.

This is so stupid...

...feeling so silly, losing the ability to think about anything but kissing the man, and having him kiss her back. But somehow, years before, she'd been able to get her brain programmed to say *no*, no matter what her body was thinking—or rather, wasn't.

Man, was he going to be disappointed.

CHAPTER EIGHTEEN

They'd wasted time—precious time. They'd had an entire week, now they had but a night and a day.

Heathcliff tossed his second boot aside and reclined next to Brianna, trapping her between himself and the high end of the lounge. Protecting her from the heat of the fire, but determined to keep her warm just the same.

Behind the fog of passion, there was a wary look in her eyes that told him she would not lie with him willingly. He wished she knew him well enough to trust him, but she would soon enough.

Did he know her enough to trust her? Of course he did. She'd been in his keeping for over a week and except for that business in his room, she'd never behaved as a sneak thief. He trusted her with Angeline, so he could trust her with anything. Even his heart.

He rolled toward her, pressing his body against her, and just as expected, her hand came up to his chest, not in a caress, but in order to stop him. But he would woo her with words, not kisses. She already knew, from their Christmas kiss, they were well matched.

He scooted back one inch, then two, but no more before he decided a kiss was a grand way to start the conversation. She must have thought the same as she gifted him with a wee smile just before their mouths met.

The press of her hand lightened, but he moved no closer. Moments later, an eternity cut short, he ended the kiss and rolled onto his back, pulling her to his chest as if he'd just finished claiming her for his own.

"So," he said, his voice gruff in his own ears. "Tell me of this Heathcliff and Catherine."

"Wuthering Heights," she croaked, then cleared her throat. "The book, it's called Wuthering Heights."

"Will ye tell me that tale?"

She took a deep breath and relaxed against him. Even she couldn't deny they fit perfectly.

"I'll try. I mean, it's basically a love story."

Her fingers began drawing invisible lines on his shirtfront, weaving around the buttons, numbing his skin and setting it afire at the same time. He had to struggle to listen to the telling.

"Mr. Earnshaw finds this boy, named Heathcliff, living on the streets and brings him to his country home. The guy's son gets really jealous. Heathcliff and the daughter, Catherine, become good friends. When the dad dies, the son, now the master of the house, starts treating Heathcliff like a servant and makes him start working in the fields and stuff. But Catherine doesn't seem to mind that he's no longer her equal, and he loves her for that.

"The complications start when Catherine gets hurt and ends up staying at a neighbor's house while she recuperates. While she's there, she starts learning how to act like a lady, and she turns into a bit of a snob. Then, when she goes back home, she starts treating Heathcliff badly, which was really mean of her since he's been going out of his mind worrying about her and getting jealous of the neighbor, who also likes Catherine.

"So of course, Heathcliff turns mean."

She paused in her telling, and Heathcliff wondered if she was making some connection between his own terrible treatment of her and the actions of this fictitious

Heathcliff. No doubt she worried that he might revert to that distrusting ogre she'd met when she arrived.

"There is no excuse for such behavior," he said.

"Oh, but there was." She paused again. Was she trying to tell him that she understood and forgave him?

"To which Heathcliff do you refer, Brianna?"

He stilled his muscles, resisting the urge to squeeze her tighter to him, to influence her answer.

"Get over yourself. Do you want to hear this story or not?"

"The story, if you please. We can discuss our own story afterward."

Our own story. He liked the sound of that, nearly spoke the words aloud again, but bit his tongue and waited for her to remember where she'd left off.

"Well, Catherine got meaner too. She decided Heathcliff was below her, so she married the neighbor. Heathcliff was in hell. Catherine died in childbirth—"

"This is what ye call a love story?"

"Well, I didn't say it was a fairy tale," she said. "But it didn't end there. Catherine haunted Heathcliff after she died. She haunted the moors, where they used to play."

He snorted. "Not terribly romantic. I do not care for this woman. If she'd but married Heathcliff, she may not have died in child bed. God punished her for punishing him. Make that a lesson to ye, lass. Never think to punish anyone named Heathcliff."

She laughed and her tickling fingers stopped. He was both relieved and disappointed.

"But tell me, Brianna, what is so romantic about this tale?"

"Well." She drew the word out and left him anxiously awaiting her next words. "I guess Catherine wasn't a terribly romantic character. Not really bright. Or maybe the writer didn't want us to like her very much. But Heathcliff's love for her was...intense, consuming. It ruled every decision he made. When she said he wasn't good enough, he ran off and made himself a success. When she was mean to him, he was mean to everyone else, but only because his heart was broken. He couldn't see straight. Completely not his fault. He just had poor taste in women.

"But in the end, when he died, he was reaching out for her ghost. He froze to death, or died of a broken heart, begging her ghost to come haunt him. And after he was buried next to her, their ghosts ran around on the moors, together."

She sighed.

"I believe I would prefer a fairy tale. Could you not recite one of those? I would end this night with something cheerful on my mind. I dare say it would be a fine change."

"You don't usually have something cheerful on your mind when you go to bed?"

"The onerous life of the laird of the manor, and some such. I don't usually have someone else to speak with in the evening. I would make the most of it, ye ken?"

"Oh," she said, and perhaps the disappointment he heard was of his own making. "Well, I guess I can stay up and talk for a while."

"So, give us a fairy tale."

"Why don't you tell me a story instead, since I just proved I'm not a very good storyteller."

But it wasn't his own voice he was wanting to hear.

"What I should prefer," he said, "is to hear a romantic tale—something more romantic than two people able to come together in all happiness only after they are ghosts upon the moors." He cleared his throat, then took a deep breath and pressed on, damn the consequences. "Have you a tale about a woman who falls immediately in love with a Highland laird and forgives him for his bumbling ways?"

The woman lay deathly still against him. He forced himself to breathe as he usually breathed, but it was hardly easy. After a moment, he could stand the silence no more, but was unwilling to change the subject. He'd be damned if he'd pretend the words had never come out of his mouth. He was finished pretending.

"Or," he said, "would you care to hear the story of a simple Scotsman who falls in love with an American woman in the space of a mere week?"

"I wouldn't buy that kind of story," she murmured. "No one really falls in love that fast, right?"

"Truly? I have little experience in such matters. But I fear it is possible for a man to love a woman in a day, even if it takes him the better part of a week to acknowledge it."

Of course he was a fool to speak to her of his feelings again so soon after he'd promised to move slower. But in the space of a day, she might be gone from his life forever, and he would not let his pride stand in the way of speaking his heart now. If he was to return to his lonely existence, he did not wish to add the burden of regret. And if he did not take advantage of every moment left to them, the regret of it would haunt him to the grave.

Like the ghost of Catherine.

"I did not wish to frighten ye, Brianna." He tried to pull back from her, so he could look at her face, but she held tight to him, no doubt to prevent him from doing just that. "Speak to me, lass. Please. Even if you laugh at me, I would prefer it to silence."

She cleared her throat. "I thought I was in love a dozen times, before David Wordsworth. But I think those were all just obsessions. Falling in love was an exciting hobby when I was a teenager, you know?"

"But this David was not an obsession?" His stomach turned at the thought of Brianna in love with someone else. But he would hold his tongue. If she were in love with the man, he had but a day to win her heart away. He would need to try harder, dig deeper for what few charms he might find in the dusty recesses of his own soul.

And what if he failed?

He let the thought wash over him, waited for alarm to squeeze his chest. It was not unlike tossing a blanket on an un-broken horse, to see if it would panic. But instead of balking, his heart assured him Brianna Catherine Colby belonged at his side for the rest of his days. Marrying an American was less a sin than being a witch. And if she chose to remain, there would be no need for unnatural storms.

But could he win her from this David?

Her voice pulled him from his musings.

"David wasn't quite an obsession. He was different. In the beginning, I thought he was just a quiet guy who needed a little cheering up. Then I got to know him, got to know how smart he was, and whenever I saw him, my heart would race."

"I can sympathize."

Her hand moved over his heart and held there, as if she were verifying that his heart was indeed racing. Then she pulled her hand back. But at least she would know he spoke the truth.

"You wanna hear something funny?" she asked. "I came to Scotland to get David out of my system. As it turns out, my heart wasn't racing because I was in love with him, but because I was intimidated by him. I was always afraid I wouldn't measure up, that I would do something dumb, that if I wasn't careful about every word I said, he'd realize I wasn't as smart as I was pretending to be."

Heathcliff's chest inflated with joy and he held his breath, to prolong the feeling.

She didn't love David!

"The worst part was that I changed my opinions to match his. He thought my career choice was a waste of my brain. Of course I took that as a compliment—he thought I was smart. So I started looking at changing my major, started looking at my time at the deaf school as just a day job to help pay for my degree. I started thinking I didn't want to be there, like it was...beneath me. I know that sounds terrible."

"It sounds like that other Catherine—the one we doona care for."

She pushed up onto her elbow and looked down at him. "Exactly! I was turning into someone I didn't like. But I didn't realize it until my family held a David Intervention for me."

"A David Intervention? What is this?" It sounded a bit like winning her heart away from the other man, something he would be happy to repeat if necessary, before midnight on the morrow.

"They reminded me what I used to be like. They showed me pictures of kids I've helped over the years, the kids that made me love my job. They told me what they didn't like about the person I'd become.

"So I dumped David—which was the scariest thing I've ever done in my life. I don't think he cared much, one way or the other, which just proves how little I'd really meant to him in the first place. But the hardest thing is trying to wash all of David's opinions out of my brain, to wash his personality out of my own, you know? So I thought a vacation out of the country would help with that. I was getting tired of my family trying to help me. It was something I needed to do by myself. So here I am."

"I cannot help but be grateful for whatever it was that led ye to my door, Brianna. Even a mad coachman."

She tortured him with silence, hovering over him, looking him in the eye but saying nothing.

"Yeah, well, I guess I can't be too mad either," she finally said.

He prepared himself for the declaration he knew was on the tip of her tongue.

"It won't make much difference, though, will it?" He barely heard her whisper, but he'd followed her lips well enough.

"I doona understand, lass. Love makes all the difference in the world, surely."

She sat up, away from him. She was preparing to run from him again, but he couldn't let her. They would finish with all this foolishness and set things right between them. He refused to suffer through another silent day.

He sat up and placed his feet on the floor. She breathed slow and steady, like a cornered rabbit. Then she gave a little laugh.

"All the difference in whose world? Yours? Mine? How we feel about each other won't matter if we're 200 years apart, will it? What happens when I go back?"

"Go back?" His body rose with his frustration, but once on his feet, his frustration went on without him, exploding out his mouth. "Go back to the year 2012? You're out of your beautiful mind, lass. Ye've had some accident, had some unhappy experience that made ye believe such nonsense. Of course yer not from the future. I'm sorry, lass, but yer no'. 'Tis impossible!"

She was strangely calm in the face of his ranting.

"So you were just playing along this morning, when you wanted to talk about the year I came from? Nice. You were sucking up so you could what? Earn another kiss?"

The memory of his grandmother tapped him on the shoulder to remind him that nothing was impossible, but he ignored it. There was too much at stake.

He dove to his knees before her and brought his hands together in supplication.

"Please, Brianna. Please believe that ye'd be happy here, with me. Stay with me. Let me love ye. Doona think to leave me, lass." He opened his hands. "Me hearts just here, in these to hands. Take it. Take it."

She shook her head. "You really don't believe me."

"My love—"

"Don't!" She jumped to her feet. Her eyes were filling with tears. "Don't you dare say that. You don't know me. You don't trust me, so you sure as hell can't love me."

With his empty hands still raised, he stepped toward her. She recoiled, so he stopped. If he took another step, she would run. He had to hold her attention.

"Am I obsessed by the thought of ye? Aye, I am. Intimidated? That too. But my heart was not racing in my chest because I fear ye, Brianna. I only fear ye mightn't feel the same for me." He lowered his hands. "I shouldn't have teased ye, this morn. It was a poor jest to goad ye into breakin' yer silence. Forgive me. Forgive me and offer me but a wisp of hope to take with me to my bed. Tell me you feel something for me, that if... If we must part on the morrow, that you will miss me, at the very least. Mm?"

She blinked and tears poured from her eyes. She shook her head, but he knew it was a lie. Her feelings for him ran as deep as did his. She would miss him if they parted. And she'd share the same regrets if he allowed her to run away now.

He gave her a sad smile. She slipped sideways and bolted. He'd reached for her hand, but she'd been too quick. He ran after her. When she realized he was on her heels, she squealed, but did not falter. She took the steps two at a time. He took them three. He dared not reach for her, lest she stumble. He allowed her the lead only until they were out of danger, then he headed her off when she turned toward the child's bedchamber.

He grasped her by the shoulders and in one fluid movement, as when they'd danced, he spun her further down the hall and up against the wall. The light from a sconce lit the top of her head. Her blond tresses tumbled from their nest at the back of her head while they both caught their breath. It took all his effort to keep from stealing that breath away again with a kiss, especially when she continued to look at his lips, then his eyes, then back again.

Eventually, he released one shoulder and held his palm to her cheek, demanding her complete attention.

"Does it matter?" he whispered. "Does any of it truly matter? Whatever I was but a week ago, I am no longer, lass. I will not be content to watch life from my tower window and remain apart from it, not when you could be that life."

She dropped her chin and sobbed as he wrapped his arms carefully around her. He was happy to hold her straight through the New Year if need be and ignore anyone who came to his door. But something was wrong; she was shaking her head.

"Your life? Your Nineteenth Century life?" she whispered, though she would not look at him. "You're out of your mind. You can't want a wife you can't believe. A wife you think is crazy." She wiped her tears on her shoulder, but she didn't push him away. "So, yes, it matters." Finally, she looked up at his face. "But if you want to pretend, for one more day, for the sake of Angeline, I'll pretend too. You can keep pretending you love me. I'll pretend I believe you."

She had no need to push him away then, the distance between them stretched without him taking a step. His chest burned as if she'd branded the words across it, *I'll pretend I believe you.*

When he'd given her that same promise, had she suffered the same pain?

Impossible. I gave the promise days ago—a lifetime ago. She had no tender feelings for me then. Then the pain delved deeper. *Likely, she has no such feelings for me now.*

What a fool. He'd wanted so badly for her to feel as he did that he'd convinced himself of the truth of it. The pain in her eyes had only been from his lack of trust, not because her heart was breaking...as his was.

He reached for her face again and when she did not resist, he held it a moment, then another still, but the futility of reaching for her soul became bittersweet. Finally, he could stand no more of it. After brushing the wetness from the still wet cheek, he dropped his hand to his side and smiled.

"Go, now. Sleep. We shall pretend tomorrow will be a fine day, aye?"

The candle he left with her. He needed no light to guide him down the dark hall. The door to his sanctuary opened without thought. As he closed it behind him, the chill air moved against his skin. Silently, he willed it to sink through his heart.

CHAPTER NINETEEN

Bree watched the shine on the backs of Heathcliff's boots as he moved away from her into the shadows. When he turned at the end of the hall, he didn't glance back.

If he hurt half as bad as she did, she was no better than that other Catherine and she deserved her pain. What she didn't deserve was her Heathcliff. And what had he said? If Catherine had just married Heathcliff, as she was supposed to, she might not have died in childbed. If she'd have just taken what was offered...

But she couldn't take what was offered because someone was going to pull the rug out from under her little fantasy here.

Yes, she loved him. Yes, she could jump into his arms and tell him it was all going to be all right. And maybe no one would come at midnight. Maybe she could just bide her time until the day he finally believed she couldn't possibly be from his century. They could work it out later.

But they weren't the only people in the world. Out there, somewhere, were her parents and her friends who were probably already freaking out because they hadn't heard from her. If she chose to live the fairytale, they'd be the ones to pay for it. Besides the fact she'd never see them again.

She laughed. What a joke. There was no telling if she even had a choice. Going back might not be an option anyhow.

The coachman would come. He had to come. He had to be the key to all this insanity.

* * *

The smell of morning made her sick to her stomach. Whatever was going to happen at midnight, she almost wished would happen right away, so it would at least be over with. Instead of enjoying his company for one last day, or even pretending to, she dreaded facing him. It was all going to be just too painful, and she wouldn't be able to keep from falling apart.

She led Angeline down the stairs as usual, but she planned to go right back to the room as soon as the girl had her breakfast and her would-be father could worry about entertaining her. Bree needed to put a little distance between Angeline and her anyway, so when Bree wasn't there for her the next morning, it wouldn't be a complete shock. As for herself, she dreaded that cold turkey affect and wondered if she would have a hard time from now on teaching little blond girls with braids.

Of course she would.

Tears were already shimmering in her eyes by the time they reached the bottom of the stairs.

"In here!" Heathcliff's voice called from the parlor. "Come. Break yer fast," he said cheerfully.

Three chairs sat around a small table in the middle of the room. The fire was giving off a lot of heat making Bree wish she hadn't put a sweater on. She'd dressed in her own clothes, prepared for travel. She wore her ragged jeans, her red rain boots. Her coat was draped across her suitcase just inside the bedroom, ready to go at a moment's notice.

But speaking of notice, Heathcliff acted like he barely noticed her at all. He fussed over Angeline, pulled out her chair and showed her how to place her napkin across her lap. Then he pulled out Bree's chair and left it for her, returning to his own side of the table so he could serve the child. If he had any comment on how she was dressed, he kept it to himself, but she doubted he'd even glanced her way.

"I forgot something upstairs," she murmured as she turned and headed for the door.

"Coward," he said, then started chattering to Angeline about why she needed to eat all the different things he'd prepared for her breakfast.

Bree's feet slowed while she swallowed a pain in her throat, then she realized that all her crying the night before was what made her throat sore in the first place.

Why was he goading her? Was he aching to pay her back for embarrassing him the night before? Or was he just trying to keep up the pretense for Angeline? Either way, it didn't matter. She didn't care what she'd promised; she couldn't bear to make small talk, and she was already headed up the stairs.

A few minutes later, there was a firm knock at the door. She stared out the window. The snow had stopped.

"I'll just leave your meal out here then, shall I?" Something slid along the floor near the door, then his footsteps moved away.

An hour later, he knocked again.

"Brianna? Miss Colby, will you not eat something at least?"

She rolled over and pulled the blankets over her. Napping was an excellent way to make the time pass faster. Too bad she couldn't get to sleep. She had no idea how long he lingered before leaving her alone again.

The third time he came, she heard his first stomp at the bottom of the stairs and every step he took after that.

He pounded only once. "Brianna Colby, 'tis time you stopped your pouting and came out. Think of the example you're setting for my daughter." He breathed on the door for a minute, then lowered his voice. "Come out, my Catherine. Let's not waste what's left of the day. Come. Play on the frozen moors with me."

She bawled for an hour.

* * *

The swelling had just left her face, thanks to the snow on the windowsill, when someone small knocked weakly on the door. Of course, it could have been Heathcliff, but Bree also detected the sound of little shoes. He had apparently found reinforcements he knew she could not ignore.

She was headed for the door when a note slid beneath it. In very elegant handwriting she had a hard time believing could belong to a man, it read,

Come see.

She opened the door to find Angeline grinning up at her as if they'd been playing *hide and seek* and Angeline had finally found her. The child clapped and jumped up and down, then took Bree by the finger and led her down the stairs. When they stepped into the parlor, Bree was confused. White sheets were draped over everything.

Was he packing up the house and going away?

She suddenly remembered a scene from Brigadoon. Gene Kelly's character sees the error of his ways and comes back, looking for the bridge, for the woman he left behind. Bree imagined herself changing her mind one day, not being able to stay away, but when she returns to Scotland, Heathcliff might not be waiting.

Something screamed and Bree nearly peed her pants. It sounded like a cross between a dying sheep and music. The girl squatted down and ducked under one of the sheets, headed toward the sound. Bree had no choice but to follow. When she lifted the edge of the sheet over her head, she saw Heathcliff sitting cross-legged on a pillow with a turban wrapped around his head. His robe was white and looked terribly authentic.

"That is not what a bagpipe is supposed to sound like," she told him.

He pointed the end of his pipe at a pillow and nodded for her to take a seat. The sound, caught and concentrated under the sheets, was excruciating. She found Angeline sitting against the back of the covered chaise with her hands over her ears, still grinning. The middle of the giant sheet was being propped up by a man-sized candelabra, the cups of which would hold enormous pillar candles—a chunky looking thing covered with rust and candle drippings that might have come from some ancient attic.

The outer edges of the tent were held up by a half dozen chairs and the only other interruptions in the four-foot high ceiling were Heathcliff's tall bagpipes.

He stopped blowing on the mouthpiece, but the instrument continued to groan.

"It's not supposed to sound like a bagpipe," he yelled. "I'm charming snakes!" He started blowing again, since the bag of the bagpipe was quickly running out of air. Then he raised his eyebrows and nodded to a pile of gold cords and tassels that had probably been stripped off the green plaid curtains. When his servants came back after New Year's, they would have to put the whole room back together again.

Finally, he glared at the tassels as if they'd failed to perform as expected, and gave up blowing.

"We'll be needin' new snakes," he told Angeline.

The girl forced a frown and nodded, then she grinned.

Bree couldn't resist. "I'm sorry to break it to you, Mr. McKinnon, but whatever snakes might have been lurking around here have fled into the snow to save themselves from your music."

He smiled, but he wasn't amused. He looked a little sad, probably because she hadn't called him by name.

Seeking for something that might lighten the mood, she shook his little note of truce and pointed to Angeline.

"Cheat," she said.

Angeline grinned.

"Thief," he said.

Before she could take offense, she realized his hand was on his heart.

"Unfair." She started to get off the pillow.

"Wait. I'm sorry. Dinna go. We've quite run out of games to play, Miss Colby. We were just about to start a goose chase."

"With a real goose?" She hoped not. He'd probably kill he poor thing and cook it for supper.

"Poor choice of words. We were merely about to go to the kitchens to rummage up a wee picnic."

"Food, I could do," she said.

When given the option, Angeline chose to bring their meals back under the tent to eat. Bree helped her get situated, then headed back out of Arabia to get her own food. Heathcliff was there, at the edge, to help her to her feet. Then he helped her into his arms and spun her out into the hallway.

"Stop," she said firmly, but the rest of her wasn't really resisting. She'd been in his arms enough to feel comfortable there. Far too comfortable.

"I just want to visit for a moment, while the child is occupied."

"Your mouth doesn't work unless you're holding me?"

He rolled his eyes. Okay, so it was another poor choice of words.

"Let us agree that we willna worry about midnight until it is but a quarter of. What say you? We can enjoy the day, enjoy the evening, and at 11:45, and not a moment before, we can worry about who might appear at the bloody door."

"Maybe no one will come," she said, trying to draw out the conversation just a little longer.

He raised a finger to the side of her nose. "No, Brianna. We will speculate not a moment more. If ye find yer mind wandering there, ye must kiss me—to distract yerself, of course. And *I* shall—"

She clamped a hand over his mouth, then realized what she'd done. She sucked in a breath and held deathly still. Her fingers wanted to move, but she wouldn't let them. She stared at her hand, dreading what he might do with his lips, wanting them to press against her skin so badly she could scream. But they didn't move. And he wasn't smiling.

She didn't want to look up at his eyes, but her gaze was pulled there, like he was a vampire who might be able to compel her to do anything he wanted. Maybe he was some kind of witch after all.

It was too bad the gold fire she found in those couldn't be bottled and sold. She'd make millions.

His nostrils flared, but she couldn't run. She didn't want to run. But she didn't want him to know just how close she was to melting, so she struggled to remember what they'd been talking about. Oh, yeah. *Kissing.*

"*You* shall do no such thing," she said and pulled her hand away. "You twiddle your thumbs or something."

"Coward," he whispered, staring at her lips. "Agreed, so long as you make use of the diversion I've assigned to ye each and every time ye worry over the other side of midnight."

"Fine." But he'd just made sure that she thought about midnight every time she looked at his lips. And he knew it too. She wasn't going to point that out, though, or the fact that his brogue was getting more drastic.

As she ate her lunch, she realized he'd kind of given her a gift, in that she had to stop worrying about what she would tell her mother. Today was simply their last day to play house.

Looking across the tent, she noticed shadows under his eyes, and in them.

"What are ye contemplating, Brianna?" His tone implied she owed him a kiss.

"I was thinking you must not have slept well. There are dark circles under your eyes."

Angeline frowned his way, but he laughed away her concern. "I slept." There was an odd tone to his voice, though, that gave him away. He was lying.

"I think Laird Gorgeous—" *Oh, my hell!* She turned her face so he couldn't see just how embarrassed she was. "I mean, Laird McKinnon needs a nap. What do you think?" Bree refused to look his way. Even when he laughed himself silly.

CHAPTER TWENTY

Bree woke with a start. She'd been having a nightmare about Angeline, stuck inside the tent with snakes while she and Heathcliff tried to find the opening.

She sat up and her head brushed against the drooping white cloth. Angeline was still fast asleep on the pillow beside her, and the soft growling that filled the tent was coming from Laird Gorgeous. Their three pillows were set in a triangle and he still lay where he'd begun, on his back. His turban had tumbled to the side and his dark head of hair nearly covered the pillow. She was going to miss that hair.

Bree needed to stop doing two things: imagining running her fingers up his chest and through his hair, and thinking of him as Laird Gorgeous. She closed her eyes and groaned when she remembered saying the words out loud. When she opened them, his dark eyes were open. And staring. At her.

Well, at least he wasn't laughing anymore.

The clock on the mantle began to strike and they remained frozen, eyes locked, while they counted the hours. One. Two. Three. Four. And then a pause before Bree could breathe again. They'd slept for two hours. The sleepless night before had cost them two hours. They had eight hours left.

He grinned and moved his hands. She realized he was twiddling his thumbs and what that meant. He'd been thinking about midnight. And damn it, so had she!

They both glanced at Angeline while at the same moment someone began pounding on the door. The little girl rolled over and blinked.

The pounding didn't stop, which meant it wasn't Bree's heart making such a racket. And as much as she might have wanted someone to come to her rescue days ago, she was ticked their little moment was ruined. It looked like Heathcliff was worried about more than just getting interrupted. He crawled past her with a pretty menacing frown on his face, like he was psyching up to face the coachman!

"The note said midnight." She crawled after him. "It's only four, right? It's not dark yet, so your clock can't be wrong."

"The clock isna wrong," he said as he helped her to her feet.

He pulled her into his arms and pressed his lips to hers, but before she could get her hands around his neck, he was backing away.

"Ye owed me a kiss, lass. Ye ken the truth of it." He smiled, but it was forced. Then he headed for the door. She followed in his wake since her hand was locked around his forearm.

"Don't answer it," she whispered.

"I must, lass. I'm laird here. I may be needed."

"You won't leave us here alone, will you? I can't face midnight alone! And what if the coachman—?"

Heathcliff patted her hand, then peeled her fingers off his arm.

"I will be right here with you come midnight, lass. I swear it."

He turned to go, but she could tell he wasn't eager to see who was pounding on the door.

She thought about staying put, pretending she wasn't scared out of her mind to find out that their time was up, that the old guy had decided to move up his watch so he could get to bed earlier. Her grandpa used to do that, when she and her cousins were staying over on New Year's Eve. He'd move the clocks forward so they'd all go to bed sooner. They'd be the only ones whooping and hollering on the front porch, racing each other to the cars for the one time a year when they were allowed to honk the horns.

Then, after they'd been in bed for a while, they'd hear fireworks and horns going off all over the neighborhood. They'd just assumed the neighbors celebrated a lot longer than normal, not that they'd been tricked by their beloved Grandpa.

If the coachman had really decided to come early, she was going to be pissed.

Pissed beat scared any day, and she marched up behind Heathcliff ready to rip someone a new one. The man standing inside the entryway wasn't the old coachman though.

"I'm sorry to be bothering ye, Laird McKinnon. Truly I am. But we all thought ye would wish to ken what was happening down at the inn, sir."

"And what is happening down at the inn, Charlie?"

The guy noticed Bree and tried not to look surprised, but failed miserably.

"The inn, Charlie?"

"Oh, aye. An old gentleman is there, deep in his cups o'course, so what he's sayin' is likely nonsense. We ken that. But—"

"And what is he saying?"

"That he'll be laird of the manor come mornin', yer lairdship. And so we thought someone should come up and check...on yer health, so to speak. "

"And ye drew the short straw?"

"Aye, sir. But I must say I'm happy to see ye hale and healthy and..." He looked over at Bree again and blushed. When Angeline wandered out of the parlor, the poor guy's eyes just about popped out of his head. "Cor!"

"Do ye need some time to warm yerself, Charlie?" Heathcliff's hands balled, then relaxed, then balled again. He was dying to leave.

Charlie seemed to notice the same thing. "Nay, yer lairdship. I'm fine to head back—"

"Will you saddle my horse? He's in the barn, not the stables. I'll join you directly and we'll go see what bile lies in this man's belly, aye?"

"Oh, aye, yer lairdship. But I've already saddled yer horse. I'll just wait outside." He bowed to Bree. "Yer ladyship."

The way Heathcliff shook his head at the boy, and the frown on his face, sent little daggers into Bree's chest, right around the vicinity of her heart.

A second later, the boy was gone and the door thundered shut, then Heathcliff stalked toward her.

"It's all over, isn't it?" Bree said as she backed away from him.

"I hope it will be, aye."

Hot tears escaped her eyes.

"Brianna, when the dust settles, no matter what we learn, my feelings for ye are true, lass. But..." He closed the distance with one big step and took her hands.

"But? But what?"

"But ye and Angeline must go with me now."

"We can't take Angeline out in that cold!"

His fingers moved up around her wrists and he shook his head sadly. "Nay, lass. Ye must come with me, up to yer chamber, the pair of ye. I must lock ye inside for your own—"

Bree started to laugh. It was the only choice she had, really. If she allowed herself to cry, she'd get hysterical, and Colbys never got hysterical.

"You think I'll run off with the silver? Or your daughter?"

"I admit I once worried ye might take the child, I acknowledge that. But I'd only just met ye then." Over his shoulder, he said, "Come, Angeline." Then he released one of her wrists and led them toward the stairs.

"You'll regret this," Bree said, but she went along willingly. There was no reason to upset the little girl. "If the coachman tells you I've had nothing to do with this, it won't make a difference, not if you can't trust me right now."

"Brianna, no matter what the man says, I'll return here, release ye, and give ye leave to go...or stay, but I must place the pair of you behind lock and key, to know that ye are safe from any who might come and try to sneak ye away. That is all. It has naught to do with trust. And I must hurry, now, to face this enemy away from my home, to keep him from me doors. To keep him from ye. Angeline is not the only one I fear might be taken from me, lass. Trust me. There is nothing in this wide world that can change that."

All Bree could think of, while he led her to the chair, was *what a pity their final kiss had been so rushed*. She was numb. The room was cold.

"Come, Cherub. My Angeline. Come quickly now."

He bent down and kissed the child on the forehead, then came back to kiss her, but she turned her head. She didn't want a kiss from this guy. She'd already had her farewell kiss from the man she'd been playing house with, but this was not him.

He kissed her head and the heat from it burned down through her brain, past her neck and toward her heart. But by the time the icy organ had a chance to warm, the door was closing, and that little flame of hope was gone. The lock clicked louder than ever before.

What if the coachman was her only hope of getting home again? Or had Heathcliff already thought of that?

Like a child, she ran to the door and gave it a thump. Then she pressed her ear to the wood and listened to the sound of his footsteps on the stairs. She and Angeline kept watching out the window, but never saw the horses pass.

There was only silence.

And eventually, through that silence, she imagined the ticking of the clock above the mantle in the parlor. If they tried, they might be able to hear the delicate chimes. They might be able to listen to each hour as it passed and welcome the New Year.

Instead, she built a nice crackly fire—with the girl's help of course. She didn't even care if they heard Heathcliff's return.

* * *

An hour later, Bree found herself nodding off in the chair she'd placed in front of the door—not to listen for anyone's footsteps, but to keep *him* from coming in the room once he returned. She rolled her head to get the kinks out of her neck and noticed it was starting to get dark outside. Angelinewas playing with her doll near the fire. The light from the flames were barely brighter than the dying sunlight.

A chill snaked up her back, then her heart stopped when the bedroom windows slowly opened by themselves. Outward! The shutters had been left open to take advantage of any bit of sunshine, and now the windows bumped against them as if pushed by a slight draft from within the room.

Bree planted her feet and pushed on the arms of the chair, but she couldn't get up. It was if her body was suddenly cemented to the chair. She couldn't get up to shut the window.

She opened her mouth, to call out to Angeline, but no sound came from her mouth. Surely that meant she was dreaming. But the cold air rushing into the room gave her goosebumps. And the creepy shiver she'd had a minute ago was now full-blown chills from the cold air. Her teeth knocked together and it brought her back to that snow-covered road where she'd nearly frozen to death. It was like it was happening all over again. But this time, there was a child who would freeze much quicker than she had.

The child.

Angeline turned from her play and faced the open window, her face lit with joy, oblivious to the cold that could literally kill her. But it wasn't just joy lighting her face; a bright light moved between the open panes of glass. A swirl of clouds. A shadow here and there. A hand of white fog grabbed onto the wall and pulled a larger piece of itself inside, like a big man pulling himself out of a car.

And suddenly it *was* a man, or at least it had the face of one. A little abstract, still swirling, looking right at Angeline. A foggy arm stretched toward her, beckoned her to come.

Bree screamed her name. There was nothing to hear. She fought against the chair, but it was like someone was sitting on her. Someone huge.

The doll slipped from the girl's hand, forgotten. But as the white arm enfolded her, she turned in its embrace and reached toward the bed, stretching toward the little scroll resting on her pillow, rolled and unrolled a dozen times by her pale little fingers, the yellow ribbon tied lovingly back into place.

But the white figure never noticed. It threw Bree a mocking grin and then poured itself back out the window, taking a still-straining Angeline along with it.

Noooo! She could only mouth the word.

The windows slammed shut. The shutters followed. The crack of the wood was like a gunshot in her ears, a gunshot that echoed every time her heart beat. Bree struggled against the chair again and again, screamed in silence over and over. And only when her voice broke through the spell was she able to get to her feet and lunge for the window.

A cloud could not hold up a child twenty feet above the ground!

Crying hysterically, she pulled at the latch, unlocked it, and ripped at the frame that would not open. She ran to the fireside, snatched up the poker and ran back. She beat at the wood frame, then bashed in the glass. The shutters suddenly gave way, bounced against the outer wall and back again, knocking broken glass into Bree's face and torso. But the spell was broken along with the glass, and she pushed it all away to look down into the shadows of snow on the ground below.

Nothing. Blessedly, nothing.

Her heart soared, then plummeted. Angeline was gone—taken, but by what?

Bree remembered the look on the girl's face when the window had opened. She'd been thrilled. She'd recognized this...thing, somehow. She'd gone happily into its arms, only protesting when she couldn't retrieve her scroll.

"Wake up," she told herself. Then she said it again, then a hundred more times. After all, there was nothing else to say. "Wake up!"

This wasn't real. None of this was real. She'd wake up in a minute and Heathcliff would be knocking on the door, ready to apologize for not believing her. Angeline would be tucked against her, spoon-style. The room would be cold, but the fire could be stoked in no time.

Any minute now, the stinging in her face and hands would fade. The blood on her fingers would disappear. She wiped her sleeve beneath her chin to soak up the tears tickling her there, but it came away bloody. Any minute, the cream sweater would be white again.

But the room just got colder and colder. Nothing covered the window. The fire gave up the fight. The darkness deepened around the cloud of her breath. She couldn't quite find the energy to wrap up in the blankets. She couldn't find a reason to care.

Heathcliff would be back. She needed to wake up before he found her this way.

CHAPTER TWENTY-ONE

Heathcliff returned alone. By the time he and Charlie had reached the inn, the old man was gone. Tracks had led out of town, away from the castle road, but Heathcliff had hurried home all the same. Darkness was gathering fast on another moonless night and he couldn't wait to get back to that room, to unlock that door one last time.

He urged Macbeth around the East side of the castle to get a glimpse of the chamber window as he made his way to the barn. As he turned the corner, however, there was no warm orange glow to the shutters as he'd expected. At first, he worried he'd not left enough wood and Brianna might be cursing him for leaving her in short supply yet again, but as his vision cleared, he noticed the odd angle of one shutter against the stone, the broken frame of the window, and then the fact that there was no glass in the window at all.

A great ball of fear struck him in the chest.

"No!" His gaze dropped to the snow piled deep directly below the chaos. Small shards of glass stabbed into the snow's crust. He jumped from the horse's back and looked closely. No blood. No disturbance to the snow other than a crusty edge formed by the wind.

Why? Why would she have need to break the window? His thoughts ran wild as he ran to the rear door of the kitchen.

Good lord, might she be gone? Might the old man have caused the distraction at the pub so that he might come for the child?

He needed light.

"Brianna!" His bellow echoed through the high stone ceiling. "Brianna!"

Embers remained in the kitchen's fire, so he stuck in a torch kept for emergencies. It immediately flared to life and he ran.

"Brianna! Angeline!"

No signs of snow or dirt on the stairs. Nothing.

His harsh breath grated against his ears while he strained to hear something from above.

Long strides later, he reached the door, both anxious and afraid to open it. He turned the handle, prepared for anything. But the door was locked.

He saw the old ring hanging in the stone wall and hung the torch there. Then he pulled the key from his pants pocket. Brianne hadn't realized she'd dropped it days before, thankfully, so he hadn't needed to wrest it from her in order to lock them in.

For all the good it did.

He turned the lock and pushed the door wide. When no one attacked him, he retrieved the torch and walked inside.

There was nothing left of the fire. The chill air poured through the broken window. He held the torch high and turned about. There, by the wall. Brianna!

Relief washed the pain from his chest and he took a deep breath.

"Brianna. I'm here. 'Tis alright now."

She sat hunched with her arms around her knees, her hair a mess, the sleeve of her once white sweater streaked with something dark. She rocked forward and back. Near frozen, poor thing. But that dark stain?

A fire? Had there been a fire? If so, they would have need to break the window! And where was Angeline?

"Brianna, love." He would go to her as soon as he knew the child was safe. "Where is Angeline?" He held the torch toward the window. Its light fell on the bed. There was nothing there but the wee scroll. The doll lay forgotten before the hearth. There was wood aplenty.

"Angeline?"

There was no answer.

The bed! The last time Brianna expected trouble, she'd hidden the lassie beneath the bed. He grabbed the edge of it and lifted.

"Are ye under there, cherub?"

But the floor was bare.

Brianna whispered. He understood none of it.

Surely she wouldn't have let Angeline grow cold out of spite for being locked in the room. He was mad to have even thought it. She was likely using her body to keep the child warm. God's teeth, but he should have never locked them away.

"Brianna? Tell me what goes on here. Are ye still angry with me? For certain, you did not think to punish me by allowing yerself to freeze," he said lightly.

He walked to her then. He had to get them into another room before he started a fire. He touched her shoulder and urged her to turn into the light. She resisted, but he could tell she had no child in her arms.

"Cherub?" He walked to the bed again and felt the length and breadth of it expecting the lass was there, sleeping too deeply for his voice alone to rouse her, a bump too shallow for him to see beneath the heavy blankets.

The chair was tipped on its side next to the open door. He could easily see beneath the table. His stomach turned. And though he feared there was no use doing so, he called out to her again.

"Angeline, 'tis time to come out. Let us go down to the kitchens and make a proper fire."

Brianna made a noise as if she were choking.

"Brianna? Are ye ill?" He hurried to her side and tried to pull her close. Her clothes were cold as stone and still she resisted. "Brianna! Speak to me! Tell me where the child is hiding."

"Gone," was all she said.

"What do you mean? Angeline? How could she have gone? None but I have a key." To the room, he bellowed, "Angeline, come forward this instant. We will be playing no more games. Do ye understand?"

Brianna made a strange groan and nestled against the wall as if she would gladly push herself through it. She could not look at him and when he pulled the torch closer, he realized the filth on her hands and clothing was blood.

"My love! What's happened? Show me yer wounds." It could not be the child's blood. He would not allow it. "Are yer wounds deep?"

Brianna shook her head, then lifted an arm and pointed a stained finger away, toward the window. She tried to speak, but only stuttered. She was obviously frightened, and if something could frighten a strong woman like his Brianna, it was enough to put the fear back in his chest.

"Why did ye break the window, lass? Was there a fire?" The torch was no help at all. He couldn't see her, but the scratches on her hands looked to have come from the broken glass. There was no puddling of blood on the floor. Perhaps the wind might have roused and broken the glass. But then why would so much of it have fallen to the ground outside?

"F...f...f...fog." She hunched down tighter and began chanting. "Wake up, wake up, wake up, wake up."

There was nothing for it. Brianna was making no sense. She'd obviously frightened the girl into hiding from her. He had no choice but to build a bright fire and make sense of the place.

He ran down the stairs, gathered a kettle of water, clean cloths for her wounds, and a bit more wood. Then he hurried back. Brianna had moved to the corner. She still crouched against the wall, but she'd stopped chanting. He tried to be patient and give her a chance to compose herself, so while the fire caught, he went about lighting candles in the room and the hallway. If the child had slipped out of the room while he was below stairs, or when he'd first opened the door, she'd need some light too.

"Angeline," he called out. "Ye're safe, lass. Come to me, child." Dear God, let her come to me! "Everything will be made right." He plucked the torch from the fire. "I'll help ye, love, after I've found the child."

It tore out his heart to have to leave Brianna, badly shaken and bleeding, but he feared the child might be in the same condition, or worse. Surely Brianna could move herself to the fire while he searched.

Angeline was not his tower room. He took to the roof and even forced himself to look over the battlements. The snow below was blessedly untouched.

In the castle proper, he searched and called, keeping his voice stern, the words kind. And with each call of her name, he feared she moved farther and farther from his reach. She was not in the barn, though MacBeth had wandered back to his stall. There were no fresh footprints to any of the outbuildings.

Sweat rolled from Heathcliff's hair and down his spine. He could only hope the child had found a way to be half so warm.

When there was nowhere left to look, he returned to the bedchamber where the heat of the fire fought with the night air. He went to the window, pulled up the broken shutter and tied it to its mate. He noticed the doll on the floor between the fire and the window. The little scroll, still beribboned with yellow, lay on the floor, knocked off with all his stirring about.

He replaced it, then went again to Brianna's side.

"Brianna, I canna find the child. Ye must help me, love. Where is Angeline?"

Finally, she lifted her eyes to his, just before they melted into so many tears.

"Of course not! She's not *hiding* from you. She's gone. It... He... She was taken." Her voice broke. "Out the window."

He was so shocked at the sight of her face, dripping with blood and barely recognizable, that it took a moment for him to understand what she'd said. There hadn't been a puddle because it was all soaking into her sweater. The front of it was soaked through.

"Brianna! Yer head bleeds! Come sit on the bed while I see to yer wounds!" He tried to help her to her feet, but still she resisted. "I dinna understand. There was nary a footprint in the snow, Brianna. No one climbed out that window."

"Didn't climb. Flew." She repeated that terrible groan, then pushed him aside and ran for the chamber pot. He took a step toward her, but stopped.

She'd talked of flying before. It was back when he thought she was out of her head.

Back when she was out of her head...

Back when she thought she was from the future. Hadn't her *suit case* been a bit unusual? The clothing she wore. The way she spoke. He'd had his fair share of conversations with Americans and their speech was not nearly so odd as the way Brianna Colby spoke. And this talk of flying? She was not jesting with him. One look at her and anyone would surmise the lass was frightened out of her mind. It was the least likely time for teasing.

But of what was she so frightened?

Cold dread stole over his heart. She was afraid of *him*.

She was afraid he would not trust her, wouldn't believe her. But he did trust her. And wherever Angeline had disappeared to, they would find her together. The child might not be his, yet, but Brianna was. And after finding that she fit up so nicely against him, body and soul, he was not about to let her leave him. She only needed to see how completely he trusted her.

"Brianna. Tell me what happened. No matter how odd it might sound to me. I vow I will believe ye. No matter." He handed her a cloth, warm and wet, then lifted her chin and tried to assure her, with his eyes, that he spoke the truth. "Tell me what happened and I promise we will find Angeline together."

Her nod was enough. He took advantage of her momentary acquiescence and scooped her up into his arms and sat her upon the bed. The cold night air poked at his back, but the fire was gaining ground since he'd pulled the shutters closed. Carefully, he helped lift the bloody sweater from her body. It was covered in shattered glass. The shirt she wore beneath was of a fine quality but the collar was bespeckled with blood from her poor face. He showed her how to hold the wet cloth to the wee gash on her chin.

"You can't believe me," she said.

"Aye, I can. I already do." After he picked a few shards from her hair, he dipped another cloth in the washbasin and began washing the blood from her face. As he'd hoped, the cuts there were not deep. Only one, on her chin and the source of all that blood, would require a stitch or two.

"Okay, but you're not going to like it."

"I never promised to like what ye tell me, only that I shall believe it. So, go on. What happened after I locked yer door."

"I was mad for a while."

"You mean angry? Easily believed." He removed her odd red boots and shook them over the fire, then replaced them on her feet.

"I put the chair against the door and sat it in," she continued. "Being angry is exhausting. I kind of dozed off."

"You fell asleep? Hardly a crime, lass."

"Yes. But not for long. It was just starting to get dark. Angeline was playing by the fire. Then..." She looked at the window.

"Then?"

"Then the windows opened. All by themselves." Bree looked at him, flinching as if she expected him to start yelling at her.

"My grandmother was able to move things about, untouched. There is little you can say that I will not believe."

"Except when I say that it's 2012."

He closed his eyes and took a slow breath. After a heavy sigh, he looked at her. "Ye digress."

She nodded carefully. "This...cloud, or fog, or something, started floating outside the window. Then it started crawling *inside*. I could swear I saw fingers. I know it had a face, eventually. It kind of reached out toward Angeline..." She dropped the cloth away from her chin and shook her head. "It was like Angeline recognized it or something! She just ran over and let it take her—only she was trying to reach for the scroll. But it took her before she could get to it. And it laughed at me, just before it left. I didn't hear it, but—"

He lifted her hand back to her chin. "And ye're quite certain this was not a dream? I heard ye telling yerself to wake up, lass."

"I wish it had been a dream, Heathcliff. Of course I do. But I'm still here. And she's still gone. And no one unlocked the door until you came back."

"And no one has stepped below this window," he said. "I checked the snow when I saw the window was broken."

"When the window opened, I tried to stand up and shut it, but it was like I was being held down in the chair. So I tried to call out to Angeline, but I had no voice. It was like an invisible wind was holding me down and stealing the sound when I screamed."

"A wind?" A rather chilly wind was, at the moment, making its way up his spine. And that wind carried with it a familiar tune.

Brianna shook her head. "I can't explain it."

Heathcliff was loath to speak for he might lose that tune, but he was more afraid of losing the lass.

"Ye said wind. And ye saw fingers?" He was shocked by the idea forming in his head, but he could not seem to hold it back, to keep it from forming.

"White fingers, made of...fog."

"The wolves," he mumbled aloud. "I've not heard the wolves since the storm began."

He finished cleaning the blood from her hands. The scratches there were also shallow and would heal easily. He dropped the stained cloth into the water, then he took up a candle.

"I need to remember something. Come with me if ye like, or stay here and get warm. I'll return, I swear it."

Her steps followed closely behind him. He would've liked to stop and wrap her in a blanket, but he dared not lose the tail of his thought, so he turned toward the East Tower. He entered his private sanctuary and took a familiar stance before the windows, and in spite of the cold, he flung them open, along with the shutters. He looked up to where the full moon had hung in the sky less than a fortnight hence. There was nary a glow coming through the thick clouds that crowded the heavens.

"I've not seen the moon this past week," he said. "Have ye?"

Brianna stood at his elbow. "The moon? No. It's been storming every night since I got here. I've seen some blue sky a couple of times."

"But no moon."

"No moon."

"Let me ponder a wee moment. I stood here, pullin' out me hair, wishin'... Prayin'..." But that wasn't right. He'd been pleading. To God, Odin, or anybody. "Dear God, what have I done?"

"What are you talking about? What has the moon got to do with Angeline? She is missing, Heathcliff. She's gone. And it's not like we can put out an Amber Alert on her, you know? Last seen in the arms of a cloud, flying out the window. Dark dress. Blond braids. Answers to the name of... Oh, wait. She can't answer to anything."

He noted the hysterical edge to her words and realized she needed distraction lest it get the best of her again.

"Let's get back to the fire." He took her hand and pulled her along, thinking as he went. The familiar stones flew unnoticed beneath his boots. He didn't remember the journey back to the ladies' chamber, but once there, he pulled the chair before the flames and warmed up the last female left in his care by pulling her onto his lap.

Then he started humming.

She shook her head at him, opened her mouth to say something, but he pressed a finger to her lips. "Just listen for a moment."

Again he hummed. It helped him remember the words. He'd been signing it only a few days before, while dancing with Angeline. Now he sang them to Brianna, willing her to realize how eerie the similarities of the song and their own story.

> *Let not yer cries...call down the moon;*
> *Let not yer prayers...be led astray.*
> *I' the coachman's guise, he'll grant yer boon,*
> *And ye shall rue...the price ye pay.*

> *Take back the breath... Take back the sigh.*
> *Give not yer name... Yer boon deny.*
> *The Foolish Fire...comes not in twain.*
> *'Tis the coachman's lanterns*
> *Come for ye.*

> *With hands of white...and horses matched.*
> *He'll guide thy love...to broken heart.*
> *Of measured dreams...he'll grant behalf.*
> *And take from thee...e'en the beggar's part.*

> *He'll calm the hounds... The wind he'll wield*
> *When the Moon he walks...'mong beasts and man.*
> *So be still yer hopes... Trust not the yield*
> *'Til the hounds behowl...the night again.*

"*'Til the hounds behowl the night again,*" he repeated. "I've heard the howling of nary a wolf since the storm began. Their cry is near constant here in the Highlands. The moon hangs o'er the glen below. 'Tis a grand gathering place for lonely hounds, myself included I suppose."

He laughed, though a bit hysterically.

"What in the hell are you talking about? You think my carriage driver is the moon? The actual *moon*?" She shrugged her shoulders. "No wonder you believe me. You're freaking nuts! A little girl is missing. My story is insane. And your conclusion is just a little more insane."

"Think about it, Brianna. She came to us without a voice, and yet she was able to hum that song. Do ye not think she was sent by *him*? And if he brought her, and he took her, she might be safe with him for the moment."

"Him being the moon." She lowered her chin and shook her head.

"The coachman. Perhaps he delivered ye both to me. There has to be something about this tune that can help us find our Angeline!"

"Well," she said. "Maybe you're right. Maybe we should fight crazy with crazy."

"Crazy?"

"You know. Nuts. Insanity."

"Madness, then. Madness I can manage. And this song—my grandmother used to sing it to me."

"The witch?"

"Aye," he said without hesitation this time. "Mayhap she taught it to me a'purpose.

"Let not yer cries...call down the moon. Let not yer prayers...be led astray. I must take the blame for that. Before ye came to my door that night, I had been in the East Tower, complainin' to the moon, or anyone else who would listen. I begged for help. I promised to give all I had, if help were sent to me, so that I might be able to speak to Angeline. I so desperately wanted her to be my own."

"Well, maybe she can be, still, if we can get her back. What's the next line?"

"I' the coachman's guise, he'll grant yer boon, and ye shall rue...the price ye pay. So the moon was called, and he came as The Coachman. And the cost was Angeline. Satan himself couldn't have exacted a meaner price."

"And next?"

"Take back the breath. Take back the sigh. Give not yer name... Yer boon deny."

"Okay. Now we're getting somewhere. This is a remedy, right? You just have to take back your wish!"

He set her aside, then stood and moved to the window. Carefully, he opened the shutters once again, used his cravat to sweep away the traces of glass, then braced his hands on the ledge.

"God, Odin, whoever ye are! I take it..." He turned away from the window, his face etched with horror. "But I doona take it back! I doona! To do so would wish ye away, Brianna! I cannot wish ye away! May Angeline forgive me, I canna do it! We'll have to think of another way to get her back." He sat on the edge of the bed and dropped his face into his hands. His fingers slipped into his hair and then curled into fists. "Poor Angeline! She deserves better than I. Forgive me." Then he whispered it. "Forgive me."

CHAPTER TWENTY-TWO

Brianna felt like someone had reached into her chest and ripped out her heart, only to hold it up in front of her, so she could watch it bleeding out. Nothing in her life had ever felt so horrible as watching Heathcliff tormented.

She found herself hunched over the laird of the manor, trying to wrap herself around his massive arms, but barely reaching his elbows.

"Shh. We'll figure this out. Don't give up, Heathcliff. He hasn't beaten us yet. What about the second part? How can you take back your name?" She ignored the part about denying the boon. He obviously wasn't willing to give her back, if in fact she was the boon the song referred to.

"I never offered me name to the moon. Not that I can remember."

Bree's stomach sank. She eased away from the bed. It took her a minute to be able to speak. She wanted to cower against the wall again, but she wouldn't.

"I did," she croaked. "When he came for me, on the road, he asked for my full name, to be sure he was picking up the right person. I thought he was from the tour company. I told him my full name."

Heathcliff looked more worried than ever. "Did ye call down the moon as well, love?"

Bree began to pace to the window and back again. "I promise I didn't talk to the moon. I didn't. I mean...really." But even as she said the words, she remembered the sight of a fat full moon sharing the sky with her as she flew from Spokane to Atlanta, for her first leg of the trip to Scotland. She remembered her breath fogging the glass. She wiped it away while she stared at the circle of light.

Heathcliff rose to his feet, delicately took her scratched hands in his. "What is it?"

"I'll go back to the way it was—back to being happy—or die trying." She looked up into his eyes. "That's what I said while I was staring at the moon. But I wasn't outside. I was just looking out the window."

"I think a demon that would steal our Angeline would not quibble with such a wee detail. So ye've come back, but not to yerself—ye've come back to the way it was, the way it was in 1806, lass. And ye nearly died trying."

He pulled her to him, hugging her against him like he was trying to absorb her into himself. Her jaw was held tight. She had to talk through gritted teeth.

"I didn't die, Heathcliff. You can let go of me now."

He loosened his arms, but didn't let go. He pressed his mouth into her shoulder, then murmured against her shirt.

"And yer boon, lass. Would you deny yer boon? Have ye found at least a wee bit of happiness here?" He wouldn't let her pull away. Maybe he didn't dare see the look on her face, but he worried for nothing.

"I won't deny my boon, big boy. I promise. No matter what happens, okay?"

Finally, he let her go. The tears in his eyes were different this time. Happy tears. He looked like a puppy that thought he was going to be left behind, but had just been invited to jump into the back of the truck. There wasn't a sign in ASL to express it accurately.

But then he was right back to worrying.

"The Foolish Fire...comes not in twain. 'Tis the coachman's lanterns come for ye."

"What's the Foolish Fire?" she asked, but hadn't wanted to.

"The Foolish Fire—the Will o' the Wisp. Some legends say it will lead lost travelers to safety. Some say it will lead them to doom. *Comes not in twain* refers to the fact that it doesn't come in pairs. If you see two lights, they are the coachman's lanterns and ye should not trust them."

"Too late. So now what?"

"With hands of white...and horses matched. He'll guide thy love...to broken heart."

"Well, I've seen the white hands—at least one of them, anyway—and the horses were white. We can just skip the rest of that. What next?"

"Forgive me, love."

She shook her head. "What's next?"

He smiled sadly then nodded. His hair fell forward and the shadow it caused made her move around so the fire would light up his face again. And a little voice in her head told her she'd better take a good long look, so she could remember.

"Of measured dreams...he'll grant behalf. And take from thee...e'en the beggar's part. He'll be comin' for all I have, at midnight, or so read the letter."

"Keep going. There has to be something in the rest of it. Some way to beat him."

"He'll calm the hounds... The wind he'll wield when the Moon he walks 'mong beasts and man. So be still yer hopes... Trust not the yield."

His eyes filled with pain then. Was he remembering the times he did not trust her? Or did he consider her to be the yield?

"Going to take the moon's word for it, and not trust me?"

"I doona trust that I can keep you, lass. If ye, too, are taken from me, I dinna ken if I can survive it."

"Stop that. Keep going. What's next?"

He shrugged, shook his head, took a breath. *"'Til the hounds behowl the night again."*

"So we know we're safe when we hear some wolf howl?"

"When the moon has returned to his place in the sky, the hounds *will* howl."

She marched to the window and looked out. The clouds were still thick. No moon. No stars. The wind was picking up a little and she wondered how close they were to midnight. Would the storm kick up again? Maybe they'd get lucky and the coachman, whoever he really was, wouldn't be able to get through. Maybe she could be stuck there forever.

But that wouldn't get Angeline back.

"So we'll know when to stop worrying. Great. But we've got to get Angeline back before we worry about howling wolves. What next?"

Heathcliff shook his head.

"It's okay. I can take it. I promise not to freak out. What's next?"

He shook his head again. "Nothing more, lass. There is naught more to the song."

Bree's chest constricted. She had to pull hard to get air into her lungs. Then she had a thought.

"Your grandmother taught you the song? Maybe there was more. Is it in a book somewhere?" If she was home, she could look it up on the internet. But she wasn't home.

She wasn't home. *Yet.*

She was four feet from Heathcliff, but it seemed like the Grand Canyon at the moment. They weren't even from the same time, for hell sakes. There was no way they were supposed to be together.

He must have read her thoughts, because he hurried toward her with his arms out, probably to hug her to death again. And as much as she would like to let him, she couldn't do it.

She stepped back and held out a hand to stop him. "Don't! We can't do this."

"Whatever it is ye're thinkin', lass, ye must cease thinkin' it."

"I'm thinking we're not supposed to be together. This was a fluke. This was a cruel joke by a cruel...whatever he is. Leading us to a broken heart, right? He never intended to let us be together, don't you see? In the end, we... Can't. Be. Together."

He stepped forward again, his head shaking in denial, but in his eyes, she could tell—he was afraid she was right.

She ducked away and put more distance between them. He didn't turn to follow her. His shoulders slumped in defeat.

"*We* can't be together," she said carefully. "But you and Angeline can. You have to take it back, Heathcliff. You have to take back the wish. Take it back and you can at least have Angeline. You don't need me. You two are clever. You can work out a way to communicate. Make up your own signs. You were doing just fine. You didn't even need me after all."

He didn't move.

"Trust not the yield, Heathcliff. You can't trust what there is between us. That's got to be what it means. Don't trust it. Take back your wish. And it will probably send me back." She just hoped she wouldn't wake up in that ditch again, or standing in her suitcase in the middle of the road. If she did, she'd take a chance and crawl around looking for her handbag, for the cell phone. She wasn't going to wait around for the Foolish Fire, or lanterns. She would use good old technology to save her ass.

Heathcliff finally turned and came at her. She had no chance to get away. His hands raised to her face. His mouth pressed frantically against hers and their faces crushed into each other in a fervent kiss. She finally had to pull back to be able to breathe. But before she could find his lips again, he was moving away from her, taking huge strides over to the window.

"I take it back," he roared. "I take back the breath. I take back the sigh. I take back the wish I made, the plea for help." His voice broke. He cleared his throat. "I refuse this boon! Take it away!"

He lingered there and she realized he didn't want to look at her again. It broke her heart, but she padded quietly to the door and opened it.

And the clock from the parlor began to chime.

CHAPTER TWENTY-THREE

———◦◦◦◦———

Midnight.

She'd heard the clock chime for a week and it had never before taken so long to strike the hour. Never. Everything happened in slow motion.

Heathcliff had a hold of her hand before she ever took a step into the hall, then they were there, together, taking each stair in unison. They moved like one person, looking forward, no need to look at each other. Nothing to say.

The clock struck midnight as they walked off the last step.

The first knock rang through the hall like the coachman had brought his own knocker from Hell.

They open the door together. The coachman stood with a grin on his face. He wore the same top hat. Behind him, one of the carriage horses shook his mane and she recognized the jingling. Was Angeline sitting inside that warm, comfortable coach?

"Good even, Miss Bree. And how was your tour of the Heart of Scotland? Did you enjoy it? The Heart of Scotland?"

"I don't understand."

"You wanted to know the Heart of Scotland. And now you do. It beats in yon chest, it does." The man looked at Heathcliff's broad upper body. "It beats in the chest of most Scotsmen, truth be told. But this particular Scotsman needed your expertise, you might say."

He addressed Heathcliff.

"And you, sir. You got what you asked for, did you not?"

"I asked for help, to communicate with m' new daughter, but ye took her away, ye bastard. How dare ye? Where is my child?" Heathcliff shook, but held his ground. Bree was surprised he didn't try to jump on the man and beat a confession out of him. But then again, he probably wasn't a man at all. And who knew what he'd do if they pissed him off?

"Well, as to that," the old man's smile slipped. "Ye were told she was yers for the now. Ye were not told she would be yers for all time. Besides, the child is mine and not truly a child at all. She couldna speak because she is a moon child, ye see."

Heathcliff's hand squeezed hers in a bruising grip and she knew exactly what he was thinking. Angeline was okay. She didn't belong to him anymore, but she was okay. And if Heathcliff wasn't going to fall apart, neither would she.

"And who are you supposed to be, The Man in the Moon?" Bree couldn't help but sneer. It was just so ridiculous! She couldn't believe she was standing there with two other adults having such an impossible conversation.

"Did I not give ye leave to call me such?" The coachman turned back to Heathcliff. "And now, the piper must be paid, good sir."

"But I didn't ask for help until after ye'd already given her to me. If she'd never come, I would have never needed the help. Ye were scheming to drive me mad all along!"

"Oh, ye've asked me for many a thing o'er the years, young Heathcliff, but what ye truly wished for, ye still hold in your hand."

Bree looked down, but the only thing Heathcliff was holding was her fingers. At least it looked like he was— her fingers were so numb from holding on so tight, she couldn't feel much.

As if he'd just stepped onto a stage, the coachman sang the song again. When he was finished, he looked disappointed, like he'd expected them to break out in applause.

"Well, lassie, ye got your Christmas kiss. Ye got to be appreciated for the gifts ye possess. Ye saw the Heart of Scotland. Now you must hand it back."

Heathcliff pulled her hand against his chest and looked into her eyes. "No. Stay, Brianna. Stay."

The old man laughed. "She canna stay, good sir. There is no choosing to be done here."

"Ye have taken my child." His voice broke. She knew how it must be killing him to be told Angeline could never be his. "Ye have taken my child, now ye would take Brianna as well? What kind of monster are ye?" Heathcliff's voice boomed across the cold courtyard. If Bree were the coachman at that moment, she would have run like hell.

Instead, the old man snorted and rolled his eyes, then looked back at her.

"The only question left for you, lassie, is this. Did you go back to being happy?"

It was a trick question, it had to be. If she answered wrong, she might just drop dead. *I'll go back to being happy, or die trying.* "Yes, I went back to being happy, okay?"

"Fine then. That's fine then. I have a reputation to maintain, you understand. Satisfaction guaranteed and all that."

"Give him back his child," she said.

"Does he have a child, then?" The old man's eyes twinkled and it wasn't in a jolly-old-Saint-Nick kind of way, either.

"Angeline," she said.

The old man rolled his eyes and dismissed her question with a wave of his white glove. "Are you not getting cold out here? Ye've not much on."

And suddenly, her suitcase was next to her with her coat laid across it as she'd left it upstairs.

She rocked back on her heels in shock. Heathcliff put an arm behind her to steady her, like he was used to seeing blatant acts of magic.

"A kind heart ye have, to try to keep my child warm. And ye gave her a name as well. Touching, but I assure you, quite unnecessary. As I said, she is but a moon child. But my favorite bit..." The man broke into laughter. It took a minute for him to be able to speak again. "My favorite bit was when ye tried to convince herself, and the lass, that ye were a witch!"

Heathcliff tensed beside her.

The Coachman, moon or not, sobered quickly. He did not look pleased.

"I lent you one of my own," he told Heathcliff. "You wanted a family. You did not specify how long you wanted one. Satisfaction guaranteed."

"What year is it?" Bree asked to distract them both.

"Here? Now? No year." The man was back to grinning, and as infuriating as that was, it was better than him being angry with Heathcliff.

"No year? I thought it was 1806," she said.

"No, my dear. I took ye both out of time, to give ye your wishes." He turned to Heathcliff. "I must apologize for the little ruse earlier, sending a sprite to play the part of Charlie. I used a bit of foolishness to get ye away from yer home whilst I collected my child. Ye showed every indication that ye might go out the window after her, so I thought it best if ye weren't present. I had a devil of a time keeping Miss Colby contained as it was. I could have never controlled the pair of ye."

The devil rubbed his hands together.

"And now, we can get down to men's business, sir."

"Business? You mean to rob the place? If ye be the moon, what need have ye of worldly things?"

"Oh, ye'd be surprised. Besides, it is not yer worldly things I'll be collecting this night. I truly have no wish to be laird of the manor and all that."

"Then what is it ye mean to take from me?"

The old man looked at Bree. "All ye have. And at the moment, ye have this woman's heart. I'll take that."

His eyes sparkled as he reached forward, toward Bree's chest, as if he was actually going to reach inside her ribs and take out her heart. There was something clearly wicked about his smile and she realized he really meant to do it.

She remembered the feeling from only a little while before, like someone had reached in her chest, pulled out her heart, and held it in front of her while she bled out. But she couldn't seem to move a finger to stop him.

"No!" A blade appeared out of the top of the coachman's white glove. Heathcliff had stabbed the hand with a long dagger from beneath. Who knows where he'd been hiding it? But no blood appeared.

Heathcliff pulled the blade free. The glove closed over the hole made by the dagger and sealed itself shut.

"Ye will not harm her."

"Ye mean to make another wish?"

"I give an order."

They stood nose to nose.

"And why should I take an order from a mere mortal?"

"Because we loved yer daughter."

"She had no need of yer love."

"We gave it just the same."

"Ye got your wish."

"I take it back."

"Ye take it back?"

"I do. If it means Miss Colby shall be unharmed, will be returned to her time, to her life, then I take it all back."

Bree stepped forward. "And what happens if he doesn't take it back?"

"Then I take ye. There are many moon children. None have a voice. Ye would prove amusing to them, I think."

"It is done, Brianna. I have taken back my wishes. All of them. Family. Help. I want none of it."

"Then give me yer name, son." There was a strange edge to the coachman's voice that made Bree shiver.

"Never," said Heathcliff.

The old man laughed, then began to sing. *"Take back the breath, take back the sigh. Give not your name, your boon deny.* Yer grandmother taught ye well, yer lairdship."

"She did. I'll not give my name to the devil."

The coachman laughed long and hard. "Ah, laddie. I be not the devil."

"The devil's brother, then."

Still laughing, the coachman gestured toward the carriage. Inside, a lantern burned brighter.

"I never intended to take the lass's heart. It was but a jest. The pair of ye are just so serious, it was impossible to forebear teasing." The man sobered. "But the teasing is at an end. Time to go, lass. Now."

Heathcliff's hand clamped down on her arm.

"The deal is unstruck, Laird. The carriage will return her to where she began. This little interlude, out of time, never happened." He waved his fingers. "Come."

She wasn't about to worry Heathcliff by mentioning the fact that she might just be headed back to a partially submerged car in a partially frozen stream. He would worry enough as it was. Or would he?

The man said it never happened. Would they both forget?

But there was no time to wonder. She had to get out of there and not make it any harder on Heathcliff by kicking and screaming and making a scene. He'd lost the child he was hoping to keep and raise. He'd fallen in love with her, only to have her dragged away by... Dear Lord, she was going to have to commit herself into a real loony bin.

None of this was real.

Heathcliff looked stricken. She must have said it out loud!

"None of this was real," she said again, taking his hands in hers. "Just tell yourself it never happened."

He looked deeply into her eyes. "And you, Brianna Catherine? Will you tell yourself it never happened?"

She shook her head and smiled. "Heck no. I'm going to write it all down as soon as I can, so I don't forget a second of it. I just don't want you to hurt, that's all."

"I'll cherish every pang, my love."

She clamped her arms around his neck, this time trying to absorb him, pressing the feel of him into her memory like a flattened flower between pages. "I love you. I'm sorry I never got around to confessing it, but I love you."

"And I you, lass."

The coachman cleared his throat.

Reluctantly, she let go and turned away. Just in case, she glanced at the old man to see if maybe his heart might have softened a little and he could just go away and forget about them.

"Not a chance," he said, as if he'd read her mind.

Hands came down on her shoulders, preventing her from turning back.

"Go," Heathcliff whispered behind her ear. Maybe he was worried about making a scene too.

Stinging tears spread across her eyes like someone bringing down the curtains. She couldn't see clearly, but she walked forward anyway. The snow was not very deep, and she wondered if the storm that raged around them all week had only been an illusion.

She climbed into the carriage and faced forward, resisting the urge to look out the window. She didn't want to see him standing there in agony and she definitely didn't want to see him *not* standing there. Either way, she'd probably try to get out the carriage and piss off the coachman. She'd seen his magic. She'd watched him scramble her life all week like a bunch of eggs. She didn't want to see what he might do to Heathcliff while she watched.

She shook her head. She had other things to worry about.

They'd been taken out of time? Was she now *back* in time, since she'd gotten into the carriage? Was she about to find herself in the ditch? If so, she wanted to be prepared.

The bastard started humming his damned song again, so she gave a good solid elbow to the back wall.

He laughed. Her elbow throbbed. But at least the humming stopped. A few minutes later, she felt herself sliding into sleep and hoped she would wake up somewhere warm and dry.

Of course, she wasn't stupid enough to hope it out loud.

CHAPTER TWENTY-FOUR

Bree woke in a car. It wasn't upside down or sideways. That was a good sign.

She was in the back seat of a cab, parked next to a curb at Heathrow Airport. She sat up and looked out the window at the same doors she'd come out of nine days ago. Or was she back to the day she'd arrived? If so, she was in no mood to tour the country. She just wanted to go home. If Heathcliff had been sent back to 1806, there was no use looking for him. And the last thing she wanted to do was stumble across his headstone surrounded by twenty tourists.

"Yer awake, then? Excellent," said the cabby. "I'll just get your bag from the boot. No charges, Miss. I've been 'andsomely paid, I 'ave. If I'm given a ha'penny more, I'll be forced to seek out me priest, I will, for stealing. See if I don't."

And with that, he jumped out of the car like he was afraid she might give him a tip and therefore damn his soul. She resisted the urge to ask him who had paid her fare because she didn't want to hear that her benefactor was the stupid Man in the Moon.

She climbed out and the handle of her purse slid down her arm. She should be thrilled to have it back, but she wasn't going to be grateful to the moon for anything.

She pulled it open and started going through it in the middle of the sidewalk. Her passport was there. Her folder with her itinerary and return flight confirmation. Her driver's license. She dug and dug, but found no cell phone.

By the time she looked up, the cabby was gone.

The airline took pity on her, even apologized for whatever it was that kept her from making her flight two days before. They had plenty of room for her and her abused suitcase on a plane that was leaving within the hour. The bag weighed even less flying home—no surprise there; she wasn't taking any souvenirs.

At least not the tangible kind.

She had a window seat on the leg from Atlanta to Spokane, but night was falling again. The moon was the last thing she would risk seeing, so when the chick in the aisle seat asked if she'd lift the blind on the window, Bree shook her head.

"If I open it, I'll puke."

What she really wanted to say was "If I see so much as a moonbeam I'm going to get hysterical and they'll have to land the plane on a freeway. Do you really want to risk it?"

The woman asked the flight attendant if she could sit elsewhere, then the guy next to her got up to use the restroom and never came back. So for the rest of the six hour flight, she would have the entire side of the plane to herself. Plenty of privacy for crying.

But she wouldn't cry. She wasn't even going to think.

She was going to pretend like everything was fine for the next two weeks. Then, when she was stronger, she was going to deal with everything she was leaving behind her in Scotland. If she still needed it, she'd have a good cry. And if the crying never stopped, she was going to find a therapist—someone slightly under-qualified, someone without the power to lock her away when she started telling her story.

Their story.

She wondered what Heathcliff would think about therapists. She could imagine him rolling his eyes.

If there had ever been a Heathcliff.

Nope. Not going to think about him. Not for two weeks.

She lasted another twenty seconds. It wasn't her fault though; the stupid, cheap airplane blanket was plaid! That, of course, reminded her of the plaid he'd covered her with one night when he thought she was sleeping.

She cried on and off for the rest of the flight, slightly enjoying how uncomfortable she made the flight attendants. But she paid for it when the plane descended. She thought her ears were going to explode. She wished she would have taken the piece of hard candy the one of them had offered, to help her ears pop.

Would she ever go back? If she did, would the moon take pity on her and make Heathcliff's castle appear in the mist?

"Not a chance," whispered a voice next to her, where no one was sitting.

CHAPTER TWENTY-FIVE

Heathcliff McKinnon and his castle were returned to their proper year. He knew because his servants arrived the morning after he'd lost all.

For a moment, he considered taking the housekeeper aside, or his man of business, or even the stableman and telling them his tale. But it wouldn't be believed. Even *he* wondered if he hadn't dreamt it. And knowing he would often wonder, he gave orders that the window in the first bedchamber was not to be repaired. Nothing at all was to be disturbed there.

He let the staff wonder about the Arabian tent in the parlor. No doubt they'd share a giggle when they found his turban and robes beneath. What they made of his cords and tassels, he didn't care.

What he did care about was finding something that might help him best the bloody moon. His grandmother had to have known something more than just the song. Perhaps she'd dealt with the blighter herself. He'd seemed to know of the woman at the very least. But he could not tear the house to pieces looking for it, not with the servants already peering at him askance. No, he'd have to search calmly.

Had the coachman been correct, about the whole holiday having never happened, then he would have no memory of it. Daily he wished he could forget her. Nightly, he was grateful he had not, for at least he was able to fall asleep with a pleasant thought. The *un*pleasant thoughts he saved for daytime, when he could at least distract himself as they poured through his mind.

He pretended to keep himself busy repairing this, that and the other, so when he was seen meddling with the sagging door of his grandmother's bedroom, none would think it odd. The slab of mahogany was swinging straight in no time, and when he casually stood and walked into the room, pulling the door shut behind him, no one noticed.

Of course it was his home. Of course he could go where he bloody well wished. But on the off chance he survived the breaking of his heart and found himself living amongst these people for fifty more years, he had to at least consider his reputation. And having witnesses to his rummaging about in a witch's bedroom would do him no good in the end.

None had used the room since the old woman passed, only a week after her twin sister had died, nearly seven years before.

There was nothing noteworthy about the bed, of course. The quilt was covered with tiny purple pansies. The drapes were purple as well. Even from the hallway, and after all these years, the room smelled of her, of the flowers used to make her medicines. It gave the impression that even the quilted flowers were in bloom.

Because of his vantage point, squatting down to examine the door latch, he'd had a clear view of the books his grandmother had stored beneath her bed. Of course she'd always had a book in hand. He just assumed she chose them from the library. But apparently, a select few had never been returned to the shelves.

If they'd ever belonged on the shelves in the first place.

Heathcliff waited for a telltale shiver to warn him away from anything dangerous, but he got no such feeling, not that he could be dissuaded. With a touch of disappointment, he sat upon the bed, reached down between his legs and dragged out the little collection.

Most of them were drawings. It was his grandmother who had introduced him to the pastime. It reminded him that at least he had those drawings of Angeline and Brianna as further proof they'd been there. He lost track of time pouring over the collection, remembering the items and people in the drawings and sometimes remembering watching his grandmother's hands drawing this line, or that line. Standing next to her, trying to see her subjects as she saw them. Amazed that he did not see the lines on a face that Grandmother somehow saw.

At long last, he had but one book left. As he reached for the cover, those chills struck him on the back of his head and poured down his spine. But he did not stop. He'd dealt with the devil; there was little that could spook him now.

It was another collection of drawings, but these were small, random. A leaf here. A bug there. A remedy for red skin. Directions for drying a certain herb, for crushing another. No doubt the local doctors would be amused. No doubt the village gossips would see it all as proof Grandmother was a witch.

Halfway through the text, the pages fell open to a chart, a calendar of sorts illustrating the different phases of the moon. But at the bottom of each phase, there were odd notes.

Never plant here.
Never reap here.
Decide nothing this day.
A fine day for crying.

If he chose to ignore that generous flow of chills he'd been subjected to when opening the book,

Heathcliff knew, in his bones, there was something important here. Something on that chart was the key to his happiness, written in the loving hand of his grandmother.

He began once again at the top.

At mid-month, under a blank square, beneath the notation *New Moon*, there was an odd comment.

He'll be about.

Heathcliff's belly burned. That was it. All he needed to know.

He was a breath away from thanking his grandmother aloud when he thought better of it. Best to keep one's thoughts to oneself, lest the devil be listening.

CHAPTER TWENTY-SIX

Bree was in no mood to go back to work. After telling her family she'd been in a terrible accident in Scotland and nearly died, they didn't push her. The vice-principals at the deaf school weren't nearly as understanding. They called every day, and she would have ignored them without any guilt whatsoever if it weren't for the fact that Shelly and Charlotte were also her best friends.

First, they tried reason. Since she wasn't suffering from any physical injury, she should return to work to get her mind off the disastrous vacation. Bree insisted she needed a few weeks to wrap her head around things, then she'd come back.

Then they tried guilt. The children were asking for her. They wanted to tell her about their Christmas vacations and she'd better hurry before they forgot about them. Bree argued that no one forgot about Christmas, even if they wanted to...

Then they tried blackmail. Bree had taught a mute girl a long time ago and her father now wanted to make a large donation to the school. She had to at least show up for the gala in his honor since Bree was the reason his daughter had found her voice. While the story was gratifying, it only reminded her of Heathcliff and

Angeline—a memory she wanted to avoid for the time being. But she couldn't risk ticking off the rich father and giving him a chance to change his mind, so she agreed to go. Besides, she might not be ready to go back to teaching quite yet, but she remembered who she was and her true calling in life. That was worth a little celebration at least.

Her give-a-shitter was fixed. But now her eyes were defective, leaking all over the place at the drop of a hat. She just hoped she could compose herself long enough to get through the gala without drowning anyone.

Her parents were rather proud and insisted on going along. When her mother came out of her room, she frowned awkwardly, like she was trying to keep from creasing her makeup.

"You're not going to wear sunglasses are you? It's dark outside."

Bree bared her teeth at her reflection in the entry mirror and wiped her red lipstick off a tooth. She softened the look a little to smile at her mother.

"Rays from the moon give me a headache. Migraines, I guess, from the accident."

She used the word *accident* like a passkey. It got her mom to take a step back and give her a little room to recover. The woman didn't need to know it was her heart that needed recovering, not her body. The look her mother gave her that night, however, promised that passkey wasn't going to work much longer. But Bree was safe for the moment; the woman wouldn't let anything ruin an important event. One would think Brianna Colby had been nominated for an Oscar.

Tomorrow, her sunglasses would probably wind up missing and it would serve her right. She needed to stop pushing her mother away. She needed to move on. She just couldn't imagine how.

Mother got in the backseat with her. "I don't want you to have to sit back here alone," she said.

Bree was pretty sure Mother was pretending they had a chauffeur—Bree would put her mom's delusions of grandeur up against the finest. Dad kept rolling his eyes and winking at Bree in the rearview mirror. He was probably thinking the same thing.

The gala was being held at the art gallery next door to the school and when he pulled up in front of the doors, he jumped out and ran around to open Mom's door. Bree played along too, scooting across the seat to follow her out.

"Very red carpet, darling," her dad whispered in her ear. "You've made her night."

Tears sprang to Bree's eyes unexpectedly—which she totally should have expected. Any emotion at all brought on tears, even if she was just happy her mom was happy.

"Stop that," her mom whispered and slipped her hand around Bree's elbow. "Cry tomorrow. All you want. But tonight, you're a Colby."

And whether it was due to a lifetime of training or her willingness to keep up the pretense for her mom, Bree swallowed her tears and straightened her spine. Together, the Colby women teetered on high heels and took their good pearls on a grand circuit of the gallery.

"Bree!" Charlotte tried to pull her aside, but Mother wasn't about to let go of her. It was a control thing, but Bree realized it was just another of her mom's delusions. On the inside, Bree was in control. Whether or not she lost it in a fit of tears every night was her prerogative.

Thankfully, Charlotte stopped tugging before all three of them wound up on the floor. "Bree, honey," she said. "Have you seen the new exibit? In the green room?"

"No. I haven't. And why are your eyes bugging out?"

Mother laughed and looked around like she was worried someone might have overheard.

"My eyes are bugging out," Charlotte said between gritted, smiling teeth, "because the subject of the art is—"

"Charlotte! He's here." Shelly slinked up behind Charlotte and noticed Bree. "Has she seen it yet?"

"No," said her friend. "But she'll have to wait." To Bree she said, "We can't just leave him twiddling his thumbs. Come on."

Again, Charlotte pulled, but Mother was like an anchor dragging the ocean floor and the four of them moved sedately around the perimeter of the room whether they wanted to or not. Bree didn't care. The phrase *twiddle his thumbs* only reminded her of the signal Heathcliff was thinking about kissing her and she couldn't feel anything but numbing pain.

"Ah, Brianna." Brady Homer, one of her fellow teachers moved toward her, carrying two glasses of champagne. He offered one to her mother. "Did you hear what happened to David?"

Charlotte frowned at him for interrupting their parade, but she was all ears.

Bree could only shake her head and wait.

"Some guy paid him a lot of money...to agree to *fight* him."

"David? David Wordsworth?" Her voice was working again.

"Yes. David."

Bree laughed. "David is not a fighter." He wasn't a lover, either, as it turned out, but she kept that little remark to herself.

"Oh, he is now. He took the money. I always thought, deep down, he was a greedy bastard." Brady clinked glasses with Bree's mom and took a drink.

Charlotte rolled her eyes. "Why would anyone want to pay David for anything? No offense, Bree."

"Oh, it wasn't just for fighting," Brady said. "The contract also said he had to leave town. For good."

Bree felt a headache coming on just trying to understand.

"So when do we get to watch this fight?" Mother asked.

She knew her mom disliked David—vehemently—but the woman detested violence more. Or, maybe not.

"It's all over. David's gone." Brady suddenly looked worried. "Sorry, Bree."

Bree smiled. "Don't cry for me. I've been over him for a while now."

Brady looked relieved. "I should hope so, what with the new exhibit and all."

Before Bree could ask him what in the hell he was talking about, Charlotte had them moving again. Mother, in her glee over David, forgot to slow them down and suddenly they came to a clumsy halt below the Venetian glass chandelier in the main gallery.

Shelly dinged a crystal flute with a spoon and the room quieted. The only sound left was that of a recorded instrumental and the friction of clothing and bodies.

Bree looked around the crowd, trying to figure out which man might be their new patron. She'd interacted with most parents, so she was hoping someone would look familiar. But then her eye caught on an Armani suit not ten feet away from her. The man wore a long black ponytail down the middle of a broad back and Bree couldn't help but compare him to Heathcliff McKinnon, a man she wasn't supposed to be thinking about for at least another week. Then he turned, and she laughed. She was going to need that therapist a lot sooner than expected because she was projecting the image of Heathcliff onto this poor guy who someone had dragged to their little gala. Probably some woman who wanted to show off what—or whom—she'd gotten for Christmas.

Bree looked away, then looked back to see what the guy really looked like. But her mind was stilling messing with her. She laughed again—the only voice in the room—then felt like she'd better apologize to the guy, since he was watching her lose her mind.

"I'm sorry," she started to say.

"I'm sorry. Ye look familiar. Have we met?" He frowned at her, like Heathcliff used to.

She recoiled in horror, but her mom was there, still holding her arm. There was no time to explain to the woman that her daughter's sanity was slipping fast and she needed to run away. *Because he'd even sounded like Heathcliff.*

Bree could only shake her head.

He put a finger to his lips, like he was trying to place her. Then he smiled and held up that finger. "Just a moment," he said, then started searching the pockets of his jacket.

Charlotte stood behind her. Mother squeezed one arm while Shelly blocked her in on the other side. There was nowhere she could run. Bree could only stand there, like an idiot, while the guy closed the distance between them. She felt the impact of each step in her bones.

He unfolded the black cloth he'd taken from his pocket, then put it over her head! She didn't dare reach up to see what it was.

Wait a minute.

Out of another pocket, he pulled something neon pink. That, too, he stretched and put over her head. Then something green with little purple flowers.

"Heathcliff," she breathed. "You can't be Heathcliff."

And suddenly the room lost all sound. The murmurs that began when he'd first stepped forward were gone.

Charlotte's breath in her ear. The tinkling of music that had been playing in the background, all gone.

"I kept calling out to ye, love. Beggin' ye to come play with me upon the moors, but ye never came. So I had to come to ye."

"But how?" She still didn't reach out to him, didn't dare touch him, afraid the illusion would disappear and she'd be standing there making goo-goo eyes at a fat balding man she would recognize from a teacher's conference.

"I'll tell ye how," said another man as he stepped up next to the illusion of Laird Gorgeous. It was The Coachman!

She tried to step back, but the forms of her mom and friends were like stones beside her.

The old man waved his hand. "I've taken ye out of time for a moment while we finish things between us."

She turned to her right. Mom was frozen, staring at the underwear perched on her head, but not moving, not blinking.

"She's going to be all right, right?"

The old man rolled his eyes. "No worries, no worries."

It was less than comforting.

"You should know, lass, what kind of man would have yer heart. Laird McKinnon here is a cheat. A blackmailer. And a witch. Ye may wish to wash yer hands of him before he tries to turn your head, lass."

"Really?" She smiled at Heathcliff, knowing she was probably about to have her heart broken again, but willing to suffer anything to have another minute or two near him. She would relish every second! "What did you do to the poor old Man in the Moon?"

Heathcliff smiled and reached for her.

The old man pushed Heathcliff's hands aside. "He harassed my child, until she could take it no more. He stood at his window and called to her, night after night, that she'd left her wee doll and her name behind, and she should come and get them." He shook his head. "But I knew better than to allow the child within arm's length again. So I waited. I waited until my usual—That is, I waited—"

"Until the New Moon," Heathcliff said helpfully. "That's the one night a month when he's not expected to be in the sky. That's when he runs around and makes mischief."

The old man gasped. "I'll thank ye not to spill me secrets like so much milk if ye please." Then to Bree he said, "He used his grandmother's Puttin' Spell, placing the child's things on a chair like bait in a trap, and when I came to collect them..."

"He couldn't take them from the room."

"Aye! He'd spelled them to stay put! After telling my child they were hers to have, even if she left him, he wouldna let her have them."

"No. I wouldna let ye have them. Human hands could remove them just fine." He turned back to Bree. "And I'll un-spell them, so he can take them to Angeline, just as soon as we're finished here."

Bree's chest twisted, along with the heart inside it. It was time for the rug to be pulled out from under her again. This was just too good to be true. It couldn't be real!

"Before you go," she said. "I want you to know you were right. I did miss you. I still do. I'm never going to get over you, Heathcliff McKinnon."

He pulled her into him then and kissed her as if he'd been waiting hundreds of years for the chance. But before she could pretend, even for a second, that nothing existed beyond that kiss, the old man was clearing his throat.

"I'm sorry, Brianna Catherine Colby," murmured Heathcliff. "That is not good enough." Then he kissed her again.

She pulled back and ended the kiss. "How can I do better? What can I do that would be good enough?"

Heathcliff frowned. "Careful, lass. Be makin' no more deals with the likes of him. He's just given ye back yer name. He has no power over ye unless you give it."

She nodded. He was right. Of course he was right. But if there was some way—

The old man laughed.

She looked into Heathcliff's eyes, trying to memorize this modern version of him to tuck next to the rest of her memories. But if she didn't try to find a way for them to be together, she'd never forgive herself. "What now? Can't we think of some way—"

"Come with me, love." Heathcliff smiled and took her hand, then led her through the maze of unmoving bodies, through the gallery.

She really loved that smile. It was full of hope. She only hoped she wasn't imagining that hope. Real or not, it was making it impossible for her to take a deep breath.

At the back, they headed for the doorway that led to the green room. Twice a year, the gallery allowed the school to use that room to display the artwork of the deaf and blind students. The room was dim as most of the lights were focused on the drawings on the wall. Some of them were framed. Others were hung as if they'd just been ripped from a sketch pad.

Most were sketches of Bree's body parts; hands, lips, half a face. One was of her calf. Some were of her and Angeline. None of them were good enough to be in a real gallery, but it was a sweet surprise anyway. There was a large drawing, a good five feet across, of a nearly life-sized Angeline, dancing with her doll. A Bree-looking woman stood in the background with her hands

clasped in front of her chest. A tear hovered at the corner
of her eye.

She remembered that day she'd found Heathcliff and
Angeline humming and dancing.

"You should have drawn yourself in that one," she
said. "They're all wonderful. You never mentioned you
drew." Then she noticed, sitting on a display cube, were
the doll and a little scroll tied with a yellow ribbon. They
hadn't aged at all.

The old man noticed them too and rushed forward
and snatched them up. The glee on his face scared her to
death, like he was about to get the best of them again!

When he turned to flee, however, his hands were
empty. The items were back where they'd started. Again,
he picked up the doll and scroll, but when he turned, they
were back on the little tower, sitting exactly as they had
been. His white gloves were full of nothing.

"Damned Puttin' Spell!" He glared at Heathcliff,
then came at Bree with one hand clawed. "You! This is
your fault."

Heathcliff put himself between them, but said
nothing.

"I've been away from me post far too long," the old
man grumbled.

Bree backed away, afraid the man might try to take
out her heart again, but Heathcliff just folded his arms
and smiled. She wished she could be so calm, but she
still didn't understand what was going on here.

"Do better," the old man told her and put his hands
behind his back.

"Do better? I don't understand."

"The Coachman can't take Angeline's things until
you love me enough, Brianna." Heathcliff's smile faded
a little. "I pray you can, for that was the bargain we
struck."

She flung herself at him, wrapped her arms around his torso and held him tight. "Please tell me that's not all you came for, to find out if I love you. I already told you, before I left. Remember?"

"Yes, I remember. You did say you loved me. But do you love me *enough*—enough to stay with me for always? Enough to be my wife? Because if you doona, the night will be short one moon until you do. No matter how long it takes."

She stepped back in shock. "You mean you get to stay until I agree to love you enough? That's easy, I'll just take it back—"

"Don't ye say it!" The old man shook his hands in the air. "Don't ye dare take it back. I wish to take my child's gifts and be done with the pair of ye. Say what ye're supposed to. Release the gifts. The man's heart is already yours. I've done everything he asked to bring him into your time. We've been running about for days putting things to rights. I've sealed every vow. Just say it."

She looked at Laird Gorgeous and hardly dared ask. "You mean, you're here to stay?"

He grinned and nodded. Without looking away from her, he said, "One more thing, Coachman. You've removed us from time again. Put us back from whence and when you took us." Then he whispered. "Time to pledge your troth, lass."

Since she was pretty sure she knew what that meant, she said, "I do."

"Brianna Colby, you will remove that underwear from your head this instant," her mother growled, then seemed to realize that Heathcliff was standing within earshot. "I don't believe we've met." She held out her hand but instead of shaking it, Heathcliff took it and kissed the back of it while Brianna nonchalantly pulled lace panties from her hair.

"Laird Heathcliff McKinnon at your service, Mrs. Colby. I was just about to donate a new wing to your daughter's school. Perhaps you'll be so good as to hold the documents while she and I get reacquainted."

"Oh, why, of course." Mom took the thick envelope he'd removed from his inside pocket and held it like a dozen roses across one arm.

Heathcliff turned back to Bree and pulled her gently against him. She fit perfectly, as always, and was able to completely ignore the three gasps behind her when Heathcliff bent to resume that kiss the coachman had interrupted. Her dad's laughter from across the room made her smile, but it did not break her concentration, as she realized...

...she had a natural talent for smiling and kissing at the same time.

THE END

Excerpt: GOING BACK FOR ROMEO

PROLOGUE

Castle Ross, East Burnshire, Scotland 1494

Odd.

The stone closest to Laird Montgomery Ross's foot looked to be the same shape as the hole remaining in the side of his sister's tomb, but he refused to reach for it.

"Nay. I'm not ready to be finished." Monty whispered his complaint to God, for surely it was God's hand that wrought such an appropriately shaped thing.

Behind him, one of the priests cleared his throat. Monty knew without looking it had been the fat one who could not cease rubbing his hands together, even while Monty's sister was led inside her would-be grave. The bastard had been rubbing them for a fair two days, since he'd arrived to try Isobelle as a witch. No doubt they were itchy for the feel of a woman's neck since Monty had cheated them out of wringing his sister's.

He could let the priest live, or he could be silent, but Monty could not manage both.

"If you canna seem to clean those hands, Father," he said without turning away from his morbid creation, "I'd be happy to rid you of them before I finish my task here. I'm sure my sister wouldna mind the wait."

A gasp of outrage was followed by silence, although the Great Hall was filled to the corners with his clan. Those who could not find space inside would soon enough hear of each stone lovingly placed as their laird buried his sister alive within their very hall, upon the stone dais, behind the great Ross Chair. Hopefully they would remember Isobelle's bravery and not how oft his tears mingled with the mortar.

None breathed, none dared rub their hands. How could he possibly continue? How could he not?

"Nay, I wouldna mind a bit, if you're quick about it, brother mine." Isobelle's voice echoed eerily from the tomb and she smirked at him from within the tiny patch of light the same shape as the odd stone. "In fact, toss the bloody things in here with me and I'll leave them at the gates of hell. Himself can collect them when he arrives."

Her unholy laughter no doubt had even the dogs wishing they could cross themselves, but it was music to Monty's ears. The Kirk's men allowed her no blanket, but she'd have the image of revenge to keep her warm.

"Isobelle!" Morna screamed. Monty's other sister stood off to his right, restrained by her puny Gordon husband. "'Tis all my fault. Forgive me."

Isobelle's sober face came forward to fill the hole as she searched for Morna, giving Monty one last glimpse of red hair.

"Morna, love. Dinna greet. The faery will come to make it all right again. Watch for the faery...and keep away from your husband!"

"Silence!" the robed bastard roared.

Isobelle laughed again, backing away from the hole. After all, what could the man do to her now?

Monty would not ruin her00 trust in the blasted faery, but if the creature ever placed its magic toe on Ross land, it would be dead before it ever took a breath of heathered air.

'Twas time.

He looked at the stone.

'Twas meant.

"I love you, sister mine." His words were quiet, for Isobelle alone.

"And I you, Monty. Blow us a kiss."

When he raised his crusted fingers to his lips, his palm filled with tears but they washed none of the nightmare away. He blew a kiss that was instantly returned.

"I'm stayin' right here, pet. Ye're no' alone."

"Get on, then." The whimper in her voice was slight. "I'll have a wee nap if ye'll but douse the light."

With a final wink she disappeared.

Monty reached for the stone, dipped its edges in muck, and pushed it home, breaking his heart in the doing. After long moments of stillness, his hands slowly opened and dropped away.

From the corner of his eye, he saw Morna swoon, but someone else would have to catch her—someone without mud or blood on his hands. Morna wouldn't welcome his comfort anyhow. She claimed it was her fault, but he knew both sisters blamed him.

If he'd have known the outcome, would he have acted differently? What kind of bastard would not?

There was no stopping the twisting of his face, the sob from his chest. He turned his head to the side and bellowed, "Out!"

Nearly everyone fled or slithered from the hall, all but The Kirk's henchmen who would stay until they believed his sister dead. Only then did he hear the muffled sobs of Isobelle. She sounded as if she were deep in the ground.

His heart shuddered with cold. Dear God, what had he been thinking? His plan was madness; she would never last. Not enough time. He had to get her out!

He reached for the odd stone...and was struck soundly from behind.

CHAPTER ONE

Castle Ross, Present Day

This wasn't the first time Jillian MacKay had felt a holy-crap-moment coming on. She wouldn't worry about it now, except for two things. First, her premonitions of holy-crap-moments were never wrong. And second, she was only minutes away from testing The Curse of the Ross Clan.

Jilly was alone for the moment, poised to enter the Great Hall of Castle Ross, the right heel of her green boots rocking nervously while she waited for the tour group to catch up to her. No sirens sounded. No trumpets announced that a simple girl from Wyoming was about to do anything noteworthy, even though, for the first time in her life, she thought she may actually *be* about to do something noteworthy.

She took a deep breath. Then another. Then tentatively stepped into the dimly lit Hall, turned to her left, and froze.

Holy, holy crap.

Silence stirred from its dreamy corner and rose to fill the Hall, pushing into every nook and cranny. There was no echo of her steps on the wood floor, no muffled voices of the tour group nearing the massive outer door—as if this moment was so pure, so important, that sound could not be allowed to sully it.

And all she'd done was look at his face.

Excerpt: BLOOD FOR INK

———— ✦ ————

Book One of The Scarlet Plumiere Series

CHAPTER ONE

Capital Journal, Fiction Section, Friday, February the First

A rumor currently circulates among the gentry in The Grand City that the white/blond Viscount of F had a visitor one recent morning, or rather, visitors, as the woman who claimed to be his wife brought with her a pair of identical offspring closely resembling the earl himself. Piercing blue eyes and straight white hair adorned both cherubs whose mother was blessed with the dark hair of her pure Spanish ancestors.

Not believing the woman, or his own eyes it seems, The Viscount of F shooed the little family from his noble steps and into the halls of a certain hotel where they have taken up residence until a higher authority might be able to hear their tale.

It was also rumored that the mistress of Viscount of F has moved out of his grasp as she deemed it unwise to associate with a man who possesses untrustworthy..eyes.

Stay tuned to see if the current fiancée of this poor-sighted creature is also saved from his company.
--The Scarlet Plumiere

"Well, Stanley, you can't very well sue the paper for libel when they did print this in the fiction section." Ramsey Birmingham, Earl of Northwick kept a straight face, but only just. His friend was not the first to be chastised by the red-penned writer. That he was being so dramatic about it, so early in the day, was an invitation for torment.

"But North! I tell you there was no woman. No wife. No children with my blue eyes and white hair."

"White hair, even. Not blonde." The Marquis of Harcourt, the worst tease among them, prodded poor Stanley from behind, then walked around the man and offered him a much needed drink.

"It's early." Stanley waited for someone to agree.

"Drink!" Harcourt slapped him on the back, nearly spilling the shot of courage.

Stanley needed no more prompting and emptied the glass, then stared into its empty depths. "Yes, white hair. There are no such creatures, I assure you. I've only been to Spain two years ago...oh dear."

"Well, the vixen got that right at least." Earnest Meriwether, the unfortunately named Earl of Montpelier, chimed in from the far stacks of North's immodest library. Oh, his given name was spot-on, as if his mother might have read the sobriety in his eyes the moment he was born, but the family name was far afield. Monty was deadly serious, and deadly otherwise. After having served together in France, North was no longer as dedicated to England as he was to his sober friend; if the Earl of Montpelier decided to turn coats, North would turn his as well rather than face his dark friend in any skirmish. No man did so and lived.

"But Monty, I'm telling you, there is no such woman." Stanley looked at a chair, but North shook his head, as if to say the morning's business was so serious he should keep on his toes.

Stanley straightened and lifted his chin, poor man. So easily manipulated. The Scarlet Plumiere really shouldn't have picked on such a harmless chap. North was of half a mind to hunt her down and tell her so.

"Well, the Scarlet Plumiere has yet to accuse an innocent man, even if she is a bit inaccurate on the specificity of the crime." Monty joined the rest, eyes fixed on an open volume of Shakespeare--the red leather set. He lowered his dark form into the seat Stanley had been eyeing.

"He's right, of course. Let's hear it, Stanley. What have you done?" Harcourt hooked a leg over the corner of a table and leaned forward for the details, his interest and enthusiasm more than making up for Monty's lack of both.

Of course, Stanley broke.

"I've done nothing! Nothing the rest of our lot hasn't done from time to time."

North couldn't bring himself to prod the Viscount further. The poor man had asked his three closest friends to meet that morning to find a solution to his newest problem--as fresh as the morning paper. They really should get to the business of helping the chap.

Harcourt was in no such hurry. He folded his arms and lifted a tan brow.

"Stanley, you're trying our patience. Spit out the confession now or I don't see us making much of an attempt to save your sorry hide."

Stanley flushed from his pinned cravat to the roots of his transparent-like hair. That particular shade of red may well have been the only color that did not become the over-blessed Viscount.

"I set Ursula aside yesterday."

"You what?" Three baritones in unison sounded almost rehearsed.

North shook his head. "I'm sorry, old boy. You did what?"

"He set her aside." Harcourt slapped his knee.

North turned to Monty. "He set her aside."

"Yes, blast you. I set her aside!"

Monty closed the book and set Shakespeare on the overstuffed arm. "Pardon my slow wit, but just how does one put an *Ursula* aside?"

Monty was right. Stanley--and his Winter-white hair--had enjoyed the pick of females since the four of them were in knee breeches together. Now he had *the* pick of all mistresses and he'd chosen very well. It was quite possible Stan, old pal, was the first man to actually end an affair with the woman. *Ursula* did the shopping for a new lover. *Ursula* let that lover know when he was no longer welcome. But Stanley Winters, Viscount Forsgreen, had *set her aside*.

"I suppose he picked her up by the shoulders, turned, and set her down again." Harcourt demonstrated with an invisible model, then dusted his hands. "Out of his way, presumably. Is that accurate, Stanley?"

Stanley's blush looked to be seeping into his actual hair.

"I let her go."

"Aah. Like fishing, then? You took the hook from her mouth, so to speak, and put her back in the water." North couldn't help but laugh at Harcourt's miming skills.

"Can she swim, do you suppose?" Monty's usual sobriety fled. He dissolved into laughter at his own jest, as did they all—all except poor Stanley of course.

The Viscount stood straighter, if possible. "You know perfectly well what I mean. I ended our affair. I told her she was free to do as she pleases."

North nodded and composed himself. "And you paid her a nice settlement, of course."

"Actually, she wouldn't take it. She wasn't at all pleased that I offered it."

Harcourt bent over, giggling, and dove onto the davenport like a man gut-shot.

Monty rubbed a hand over his face, shook his head, then stiffened. "That has to be it! Ursula found the Scarlet Plumiere and had you punished. Severely punished, it appears; if night follows day, and things play out the way the SP has predicted, you, my dear Viscount of F, are about to be released from your engagement."

"But that's why I let her go, you see? It would be poor form to keep one's mistress while one is preparing for marriage, and honeymoon, and fatherhood, and…"

"And death." Having solved the mystery, Monty's nose was back in the book.

"Yes, that too. If Irene Goodfellow breaks it off, Mother will have me fed to the fish, and even though she's doddering, she'll find a way to bear another son to replace me."

"It's unsettling the way that woman tosses that threat about," North admitted. "It fairly gives me nightmares thinking about it."

"Well, thinking about it has put me off seeing Ursula."

"Quite so. Quite so." North nodded, thinking. The mystery was solved, but what were they to do about it?

"It would be best to have her put down, Stanley. For your own good," Harcourt mumbled against a cushion.

"Who? The Scarlet Plumiere? I can't have a woman murdered, even if she's essentially ruined my life with her blasted article. I can't believe you'd suggest such a thing."

"Oh, not her, man. Your mother." Harcourt rolled

onto his back and spoke to the ceiling. "Have your mother put down like the old horse that she is and enjoy the reprieve. Marry in another ten years."

"Put down my mo...you're mad!"

"No. Actually, it wasn't a bad idea a'tall." Monty closed his book again and tossed it onto the table.

"All right. You're both mad. I won't be having my mother...put down, for God's sake."

"Oh, Stanley. Do keep up." Monty folded his hands and grinned. He must have had a grand idea; he didn't smile easily. "I mean the SP, of course, not your dear saintly horse-of-a-mother."

"You mean it? You can stand here in front of God and good whisky and talk of having a woman murdered? Because all of London knows it's a woman writing those articles. Good lord, man. Perhaps I don't know you at all. Perhaps you could actually do the deed yourself!"

"Oh, I would rather not do the deed myself, of course. But I suppose if I must..."

North couldn't take it anymore. He tossed up his hands.

"I surrender as well, Monty. What are you thinking? You can't be talking about having a woman murdered."

"Not murdered. Put down. Taken out of the picture--or the Capital Journal at least." Monty leaned in and lowered his voice. "The only way to control a woman these days, gentlemen, is to marry her off."

Harcourt rolled back onto his face and mumbled, "I was afraid you would say that."

Callister stepped into the library with a small white box tied with crimson ribbon. North nodded his butler over and reached for the package, but the old man shook his head.

"I beg your pardon, my lord, but this just arrived for Viscount Forsgreen."

Something yawned and stretched inside North's

breast, something that had been sleeping for years. Usually, when it woke, he drugged it with Brandy until it slept again. He wasn't sure, but it might have been his soul. And with some sort of premonition which he'd never been known to possess, he suspected that *thing* within him would somehow be affected by Stanley's box.

He watched, as did they all, while Stanley slowly pulled a crimson tail, as if they expected a cat to jump out from beneath it.

The ribbon fell away. Nothing happened. Stanley sat the box upon the table, lifted the lid, and set it aside. He frowned, looked at North, then reached into the box. He pulled out a pair of spectacles...and a bubble burst in North's chest.

He laughed.

Stanley didn't seem to understand.

"Who did you tell about this meeting, *Viscount F*?" Monty had to raise his voice to be heard.

North laughed harder. Watching Stanley's face as realization dawned, struck him as particularly amusing.

"Poor eyesight." Harcourt's grin widened further than the confines of his face. "I say, she's a clever minx."

North agreed. The Scarlet Plumiere was clever. And had he a heart, she might have just won it over with her wit alone.

Acknowledgements

Thank you to my editorial team—Diane, Annie, Marli, and Suzi. Thanks for having my back on this one! And to my fellow Crazy Ivans who push me when I need pushing.

About the Author

L.L. Muir lives in the shadows of the Rocky Mountains. Like most authors, she is constantly searching for, or borrowing pens. She manages her characters in a waiting room in her head where fights often break out over who's story should be next in line.

If you like her books, tell a friend!

She loves to hear from readers. You can reach her through her website—

www.llmuir.weebly.com

26909494R00132

Made in the USA
Lexington, KY
21 October 2013